THE SCAR

K. A. GUNASEKARAN was a teacher, folk-artist, dramatist and researcher. He was the dean of the School of Performing Arts at Pondicherry University. He was the director of the International Institute of Tamil Studies.

V. KADAMBARI taught English at the Ethiraj College for Women, Chennai. She is a bilingual writer and translator, and is keenly interested in gender issues and gender studies.

Mission Statement

This is an initiative of the Adi Dravidar and Tribal Welfare Department (AD&TW Dept) under the aegis of one of the announcements for the year 2023–2024 "The best Tamil Works of Adi Dravidar and Tribal writers will be translated into English" by Honourable Minister for Adi Dravidar Welfare Thirumathi N. Kayalvizhi Selvaraj.

The Adi Dravidar and Tribal Welfare Department aims to elevate the voices and literary contributions of accomplished writers from the Adi Dravidar and tribal communities by translating and republishing their literary works. The translated works will provide a global platform for these writers to spread their word across the world. The programme strives to bridge cultural divides by translating and republishing their books, serving as a pathway to their voices and enabling readers to enter a diverse and profound tapestry of storytelling. Furthermore, the initiative seeks to inspire and nurture emerging talent within these communities. By showcasing the achievements of established writers, it will encourage to motivate aspiring authors to share their own stories and perspectives, thereby fostering the expansion of a distinct literary horizon.

This will be enhanced by the movement of these works through the Publication wing of the Tamil Nadu Textbook and Educational Services Corporation in their programme of collaborating with reputed national and international publishers. The department strives to empower writers, break down barriers, and introduce new voices in literature to a global audience, thus contributing to a more inclusive and enriched literary landscape.

G. Laxmi priya
Secretary to Government

THE SCAR

K. A. GUNASEKARAN

Translated from the Tamil
by
V. KADAMBARI

Orient BlackSwan

All rights reserved. No part of this book may be modified, reproduced or utilised in any form, or by any means, electronic or mechanical, including photocopying, recording or by any information storage and retrieval system, in any form of binding or cover other than in which it is published, without permission in writing from the publisher.

THE SCAR

ORIENT BLACKSWAN PRIVATE LIMITED

Registered Office
3-6-752 Himayatnagar, Hyderabad 500 029, Telangana, India
e-mail: centraloffice@orientblackswan.com

Other Offices
Bengaluru, Chennai, Guwahati, Hyderabad, Kolkata,
Mumbai, New Delhi, Noida, Patna

© Orient Blackswan Private Limited 2024
First published by Orient Blackswan Private Limited 2024

ISBN 978-93-5442-862-3

The contents of this book reflect the views of the author and the translator. Neither the Tamil Nadu Textbook and Educational Services Corporation nor the Adi Dravidar & Tribal Welfare Department is responsible for the same.

Typeset in Adobe Garamond 11/13 pt

Typeset by
Trinity Designers and Typesetters
Chennai

Printed in India at
Yash Printographics, Noida 201301

Published by
Orient Blackswan Private Limited
3-6-752 Himayatnagar, Hyderabad 500 029, Telangana, India
e-mail: info@orientblackswan.com

Contents

Preface vii

Introduction x

Translator's Note xix

The Scar 1

Select Glossary 96

Preface

My early days were closely associated with the people of Islam. I realised even while at school, that caste differences did not exist in Elanyankudi – a place with a large Muslim population, whereas in places just two kilometres away, it was found in excess. I contemplated the horrid experiences I have had because of caste discrimination in my early life. *Vadu* evolved. Anger welled up as I wrote about the discriminatory practices that I had suffered; sometimes tears flowed. I have captured in my writing all the experiences that I narrated to my friends on various occasions.

Kalaikulam village is near Thayamangalam. This is where my friend Samidoss was born. I had an unforgettable experience when I stayed there one night. At around midnight, a kudukuduppaikaran entered the cheri making the eerie rattling sound peculiar to his tribe.

I woke up even as he entered the street. I told Samidoss, 'Dei! I will hide in the cattle shed opposite your house. I want to see how this fellow makes his appearance.' Samidoss warned me saying, 'He will bring the ghosts with him. He will incapacitate you.' I decided to confront him and hid myself in the cattle shed. Samidoss lay frozen with fear.

The kudukuduppaikaran stood at the entrance shouting, 'Thoo, thoo, thoo, graveyard hag.' The entire village was quivering with fear, I think. None came out. I got up quickly, folded my kaili, and walked across, whistling. The fellow did not know what to do and left in a huff without finishing his oracles for the entire street, shouting and threatening, 'Thoo, thoo, thoo…something bad is going to happen to this house.'

In Salaiyur, during Ramzan, the fakirs would go around the Muslim streets, singing to the accompaniment of beats kept by a small drum. I used to stay awake to watch them. I think it is this habit that helped me to accost the kudukuduppaikaran in Kalaikulam.

Like this, there are so many anecdotes which come to my mind on and off. There are many incidents, which have been left out. I have written about only a few of them in *Vadu*.

When I read parts of what I had written to Elango teacher, he felt as though it was his own experiences that were being narrated. Comrade A. Marx encouraged me to compile my experiences.

Comrade Ravikumar published an excerpt from *Vadu* in *Dalit Murasu* magazine. It was well received. In order to bring it out as a book I sent a soft copy of *Vadu* to Kalachuvadu.

I had the unique privilege of having Professor Nanjundan as the editor of my book. He gave me useful suggestions to bridge the gap between my style and the content. Our meeting at Salem and the discussions I had with him helped in making *Vadu* understandable to all readers, without compromising the language of my soil. His knowledge of grammatical Tamil without any formal training in it is impressive.

I have related my experiences upto my college days in this account. The experiences I have had since the time, my involvement in Marxist movements, my journey down the arts lane, do not figure in this book. Dalit youngsters who read *Vadu* may be inspired to realise that they need to fight this caste-ridden society with more energy than the others do. For the others, this book is an introduction to dalit life.

While proof reading, my wife Revathi's constructive criticism of my style of writing was very useful. To her and to Comrade A. Marx, I owe my gratitude. I am grateful to my friend, Nanjundan, Comrade P. Panchangam, Dr. A. Thirunagalingam, a friend from my childhood days (who reminded me of the many experiences that I had left out) and Karasur Palanichami.

I also thank Ravikumar for his erudite preface, and Kalachuvadu Publishers.

K.A. Gunasekaran*
20 December 2004
Pondicherry

---

* This preface is a translation from the Tamil edition.

Introduction

History, a string of incidents woven together like beads in a rosary, does not leave any trace of the Dalit people. Hence they write their history themselves. Autobiography is the consequence of their yearning to create their society's history through their individual life story.

Dalit autobiography has turned out to be not only a part of the Dalit history but also an important node of Dalit literature. Not only are they published in various Indian languages, but are also translated into English. Autobiographies of Narendra Jadhav, Sharankumar Limbale, Vasanth Moone, Omprakash Valmiki, Laxman Mane and others have been translated into English and other European languages. The autobiographies of Aravind Malagatti and Siddhalingayya, written in Kannada, are at present translated into English. These translations have created a special place for Dalit literature at the global level.

We do see difference of opinion among the critics about their response to Dalit literature. Some feel it is gaining visibility at the global level while others contemptuously look at it as a strategy of liberalisation to convert the Dalit sorrows into assets. (*Touchable Tales*, 2003) Nevertheless, autobiography as a literary form has been used all over the world by the oppressed as a vehicle to project themselves. Despite the campaign about the death of the author by the Post-Structuralists, autobiographies continue to be written.

At the national level, Ambedkar and Rettaimalai Srinivasan are the precursors of the Dalit autobiographical form as per research indicators at present. Their autobiographies have in fact come out as precise notes. Both autobiographies seem to have been written in

1939. In fact the last note in Ambedkar's autobiography gives a detailed account of an incident that happened in 1938, thereby proving that the compilations must have been brought out after that. Rettaimalai Srinivasan's *Jeeviya Saritira Surukkam* (*A Brief Autobiography*) was published by Pyne & co, Madras, in 1939.

According to Ambedkar, foreigners do know that the stigma called untouchablility is in vogue in India. But they do not know how gruesome it is. Ambedkar further observed, a dalit in a village does not socialise with others nor is he accepted by others. Despite this he considers the village to be his. Foreigners are puzzled by this. Therefore, the challenge is to give them the exact picture of how the untouchables are treated by the caste Hindus. According to him this dichotomy could be solved in two ways. One, by giving a general description of how the untouchables are treated, or two, by describing it with the help of the various happenings in one's life. Knowing that the second way would be more effective, Ambedkar described untouchability with the help of select incidents from his own experiences and from that of others.

These reminiscences written to form parts of Ambedkar's autobiography have been compiled under the title *Waiting for a Visa*. Six incidents that happened between the years 1901-38 are presented in this compilation.

It is more or less at the same time that the autobiography, *Jeeviya Saritira Surukkam* by Rettaimalai Srinivasan, was published. It is this book, which could be considered for the present as the precursor of the Tamil Dalit autobiographies.

The two books mentioned above are not autobiographies written in a detailed and full-fledged manner. The reasons for their publication were clearly mentioned in the books. Ambedkar wanted the foreigners to get the correct picture of the gruesome nature of untouchability. Rettaimalai Srinivasan's aim was to, 'Write about the little improvement that the community at present called the Adi Dravida has achieved in the past fifty years in all the so many thousands of years gone by; to draw attention to the fact that the little help that has been rendered by the rest of the society for the welfare of these people is not without self interest; and also to make clear the fact that this community of people have achieved whatever they have by their own struggle.'

We cannot classify all the autobiographies that are written by the Dalits all over India as akin to Ambedkar's or Rettaimalai Srinivasan's writings. However, in all the Dalit autobiographies certain elements that are found in the above two pioneering works can be seen. In the Dalit autobiographies one can see the inhuman aspects of untouchability. Hence it can be said that Dalit autobiographies help to promote an ideology against untouchability.

Arjun Dangle points out that Dalit literary activities were taken up in Marathi, much before the Ambedkar movement started. He mentions among the many writers, Gopal Baba Walanker, Pandit Kondiram and Kishan Bagoji Banchoth who have made significant contribution even as early as 1920. (*Dalit Ilakiyam*, 1992)

Evidences reveal that, in Tamil, such efforts were taken even before this time. Among the many pioneering Dalit efforts, only the magazine called *Tamizhan* is available now. 'We would have been much more informed had we been able to retrieve magazines such as *Adidravidan, Maha Vikatadudan, Boologa Vyasam, Parayan, Adidravidamitran*. These are not available. Moreover the non-availability of the various poems, essays and plays written by the Adidravidas for the fifty years, between 1860–1910, prevents us from knowing their history well', says Anbu Ponnoviyam, and he is quite right. (Foreword, *Ayodhidasar Cinthanaikal (Ayodhidasar's Thoughts)*, 1999)

Only the views of Pandit Ayodhidasar have been republished from the magazine *Tamizhan*. We do not know if the magazine had creative literary writings. Anbu Ponnoviyam says that some information can be culled from *Madurai Prabandam* and *Rangoon Pravesa Thirattu* published in 1896. According to Ayodhidasar's writings, Valluvar and Avvai are the ancestors of the Dalits. If their literary works, which flails against caste divisions, can be considered as part of Dalit literature, one may be able to understand the heritage of Dalit literature as being equal to the agelessness of Tamil itself.

Many essays of Ayodhidasar could be shown as illustrations for the critical views on Dalit literature. (I am also writing a book on it). It can thus be said without hesitation, that only in Tamil have efforts been taken for a critical analysis of Dalit literature. While speaking about Marathi Dalit autobiographies, Arjun Dangle terms the period 1978–86 as the autobiographical literary period. Daya Pawar's *Baluta*, M.K. Sen Kamble's *Advanin Che Pakshi*, Laxman Mane's *Upaara* are mentioned by him. After this period many more autobiographies have been published in this language.

Though Rettaimalai Srinivasan's *Jeeviya Saritra Surukkam* came out in 1939, no other Dalit autobiography in Tamil seems to have followed it. In the last ten years though many Dalit literary works have been published, there are no autobiographical writings. Bama and Raj Gouthaman's writings cannot be categorised as autobiographies, nor can they be termed as auto fiction, since 'auto fiction is nothing but trying to grasp the eluding meaning of life through one's writing.'

K.A. Gunasekaran's *Vadu* makes its appearance against this background. It talks about his life upto his graduation. Not only is it a record of his experiences, but it is also a documentation of a certain time. When talking about his father, a school teacher, struggling to give him an education; or his mother who had studied upto the middle school even in those days, but nevertheless had to take up jobs like issuing tickets at the cinema theatre, chopping firewood and cutting grass to support the family; or about how he and his siblings contained hunger by eating soaked tamarind seeds for breakfast, Gunasekaran's language touches the depths of one's heart without in the least evoking pity. We do not see in Gunasekaran's language the anger of the language of Namdeo Dhasal, who wished 'to copulate with hunger'. Nevertheless, his language instills that anger in the reader.

The autobiography evokes a mixed culture of Hinduism, Islam and Christianity. We do not see the rituals, habits and customs, which he mentions, in any of the religious texts. The rituals carried out for the 'possessed' Muslim women, the illiterate women requesting help to read and write letters to their husbands living abroad, and paying to listen to the readings on Nabi's life or to the cinema stories that they are prevented from watching, are situations which prevail in many villages even today.

We understand from this autobiography that at the economically lower rung of society, religions like Islam, Christianity and Hinduism merge, losing their identities in a very natural manner. Especially now, when identities are frozen and differences are brought into sharp focus, such efforts to lay open the reality are the need of the hour. Gunasekaran does not do it by displaying his political correctness. But just by laying bare his life, he has achieved this task.

Migration is an inevitable factor of his life, since he is a folk artist. Employing untouchability, Hinduism tries to hamper a Dalit's movement. His place of living and his area of socialising are all very clearly circumscribed. If he crosses the limit set for him he would be punished. The Dalits thus restricted, do not know any other land other than their own. It is this limitation that is the hurdle for collecting them together politically. Their indifference to what happens beyond their village is also due to this. Even now, when communication channels have widened so much, Dalits are not able to think about or move beyond their limited sphere. That is the reason why the Dalits in north Tamilnadu were not shaken by what happened in Melavalavu or Tamiraparani. So also, the atrocities committed in the north against the Dalits have not in any way affected the Dalits of the southern districts. Folk artists are generally not restrained by conventions. Hence they are relatively free. Gunasekaran is one such artist.

These artists do not suffer from the psychological fear and the low-esteem that are generally found in Dalits who are keenly aware of their marginality. Therefore, it is natural for these people to have self-sufficiency and courage as they enjoy popular acclaim through their art. They cross the barriers imposed by caste with the help of their artistic achievements. Gunasekaran's mobility is reflected in this autobiography.

The themes for Gunasekaran's modern plays are drawn from every day life. *Thodu* (*Touch*) a play recently directed by Gunasekaran is based on an incident in his life that is narrated in his autobiography. It is about a caste conscious Hindu who suddenly has an epileptic attack and is seen frothing at the mouth. Muniyandi Machan rushed to his aid, but on regaining consciousness the man upbraids him, 'You Paraya, why did you touch me?' and made him apologise in front of the panchayat. (*Dalit*, May–July 2002)

This reminds us of an incident that Rettaimalai Srinivasan mentions in his autobiography. Describing his meeting with King George at the Roundtable Conference, in England, he says, 'I got an opportunity to speak again with the emperor. He asked me about untouchability. When I said the high caste will not touch the low caste, he asked me, "Wont a high caste help a low caste to his feet even if he falls on the road?" When I said, he won't, the emperor was shocked and shaken, and he said, "I will never allow this in my empire"'.

According to the untouchability ideology, it is not that a high caste alone is not allowed to pick up a low caste fallen on the road, but it also demands that a low caste man must not render help to a high caste. Like the emperor who was shocked by what Rettaimalai Srinivasan said, is there anyone here who would be shocked by the incident which Gunasekaran has narrated? Our democrats would rather try to prove it a lie than be affected by it.

Appreciating Dalit autobiographies as works that present reality without any exaggeration, Arjun Dangle says, an autobiography is not circumscribed by a writer's life alone. It is an expansion and extension of a societal description. This autobiography of Gunasekaran has the same qualities. But the same cannot be said of other Dalit autobiographies which are translated with haste into English and into other European languages and imported with the same spirit in Tamil. There are autobiographies which are constructed on 'self-pity' and 'self-denigration' and others written on the consolidated pain of the Dalits appropriated by an individual writer in order to profit by it. However, K.A. Gunasekaran's autobiography cannot in any way be counted among those, because though he talks about himself in this autobiography, he does not portray himself as a hero. A bigger community is seen through his story. This aspect of not magnifying his self makes us distinguish this autobiography from that of the others. This autobiography bears ample testimony to the fact that wounds made of fire might heal but wounds made of untouchability would continue to give trouble. It is also in this aspect that we are able to recognise the continuum of thought pattern from the autobiographies of Ambedkar and Rettaimalai Srinivasan.

I want to point out two important issues related to the form called autobiography. Portrayed as the voice of the victim, the Dalit autobiography is a testimony and an appeal. The person who submits it does not have the right to judge. It is also doubtful if the Dalit autobiographies would remain the same if they were to take up a judgemental role. Autobiographies are written based on truthfulness and trustworthiness. They try to offer human life as a linear narrative – the present written word trying to capture the past history. They are conceived in the language of adventure highlighting the achievements of an individual, whereas a literary work is an adventure of language. This is the second problem related to an autobiography.

An autobiography can transcend these two limitations to become a literary piece in itself. In order to do so, a conscious effort is required. According to Foucault, a work of art should be an experiment conducted on one's self. Why do we write a book? The first reason is our interest in knowing new things. The second is the transformation that we bring on ourselves through writing. These words show the way to transform an autobiography into a literary piece:

Come, brother, and tell me your life
come, show me the marks of revolt
which the enemy left on your body

Come, say to me, 'Here
my hands have been crushed
because they defended
the land which they own'

'Here my body was tortured
because it refused to bend
to invaders'

'Here my mouth was wounded
because it dared to sing
my people's freedom'

Come brother tell me your life,
come relate me the dreams of revolt
which you and your fathers and forefathers
dreamed
in silence
through shadowless nights made for love

Come tell me these dreams become
war,
the birth of heroes,
land reconquered,
mothers who, fearless,
send their sons to fight.

Come, tell me all this, my brother.
And later I will forge simple words
which even the children can understand
words which will enter every house
like the wind
and fall like red hot embers
on our people's souls.

In our land
Bullets are beginning to flower.

A Dalit autobiography should be so – light as air, and simple enough for even children to understand. Yet it should fall on the souls of the readers like smouldering coal. You would know as you read if this autobiography has achieved this.

RAVIKUMAR*
Pondichery
8 December 2004

BIBLIOGRAPHY

Ambedkar, B.R., *Ambedkar Autobiographical Notes,* Navayana, 2003.
Anand, S, ed, *Touchable Tales – Publishing and Reading Dalit Literature,* Navayana, 2003.
Dangle, Arjun, *Dalit Ilakiyam,* Tamaraiselvi Pathipagam, 1992.
Ponnoviyum, Anbu, Foreword. *Ayodhidasar Cinthanaikal* (Ayodhidasar's Thoughts), Part I, Nattar Vazhakatriyal Aaivumaiyam, Palayamkottai, 1999.
Srinivasan, Rettaimalai, *Jeeviya Sarithira Surukkam,* Dalit Sahitya Akademi, 1999.
'An interview with Serge Doubrovsky', *The Journal of Twentieth Century Contemporary French Studies,* vol. 2. no. 2, 1997.
Jorge Rebelo's 'Poem' has been quoted in the concluding section of the introduction. Rebelo is from Mozambique. The poem is from, Wole Soyinka, ed, *Poems of Black Africa,* Heinemann, 1975.

---

* This introduction has been translated from the original Tamil edition.

Translator's Note

Translating *Vadu* has been as much an expedition as the reading of it. There was a continuous quest and search throughout – quest for understanding human nature and search for methods of societal change, at a time when caste and discrimination seem to be more crude now than ever before. Apart from being truthful and faithful in my translation to the source text, I have also metamorphosed and expanded myself by the process. Critics, as well as Dalit writers themselves, describe Dalit autobiographies as 'narratives of pain'. This pain, which runs through Gunasekaran's narrative is passed on to a sensitive reader even though the language is not overtly strident.

True Art after all is not ranting. It is a vision. *Vadu* is written with the vision to change hardened hearts. I feel privileged to be a tool towards realising such a vision. I am thankful to Orient Blackswan, and in particular to Deepa Krishnamurthy, for asking me to translate this autobiography. I wish to record my gratitude to Professor Devadatta, for urging me to take up the assignment. My thanks are due to Vidyuta and Vasudha who helped with the typing and for offering useful comments, and to the many friends who had confidence in me.

V. Kadambari
Chennai
June 2009

1

My father's birthplace was Marandai. Mother was born in Keeranoor. My periamma was born in Thovoor. People belonging to all these three places came to Elayankudi for the weekly sandhai. Even in those days this weekly sandhai at Elayankudi was described as the biggest market place in Ramanathapuram district. Villages such as Elayankudi, Salaiyur, Pudhur, where the Muslim population was large, were strung together in a single line by a straight road. Often one heard the nagara and the namaz from these villages.

It was in Salaiyur that Father started his career as a teacher and brought us up too. The Siva Temple in Elayankudi lay in that part of the city where the Arya Vysyas lived in large numbers. I have never been inside this temple even today. But I have often touched the four feet stone figure of Ammanavayan, sitting cross-legged in front of this temple. Later during my M.A. days in Madurai, when the professors who taught Saiva Siddhanta spoke about how the Saivites put on stake and quartered thousands of Jains, I could not but think about this statue outside the Siva temple, to whom the people prayed, making an offering of coconuts and pongal. Local people say that the Ammanavayan statue was found in the Elayankudi canal. I was again reminded of this statue when I read much later in the accounts of Rettaimalai Srinivasan and Ayodhidasa Pandithar that the Siva temples were constructed by Saivites on the sites of original Jain temples.

Near the Siva temple was the temple of the Valmel Nadantha Amman. The fields belonging to this temple were also closeby. It was called the Maranayanar field. They say Siva had appeared before Maranayanar, in the form of a Saivite ascetic begging for food, to test his devotion.

'I have just sown the seeds on the field and there is nothing at home that I can offer. What kind of a test is this?' thought the good man to himself. However, he was determined to feed the ascetic. He entreated him to rest awhile, and rushed to the field to pick the grains he had sown earlier. He cleaned, pounded and cooked the rice, and served the ascetic. This field near the temple, which is said to have belonged to him, was called Elayankudi Maranayanar field.

Every year the festival at the Valmel Nadantha Amman temple would take place. The goddess would be brought on a chariot pulled by horses. The priest who stood near the Amman idol would shoot an arrow from the bow in his hand. If it went high up into the sky, people believed that there would be rains that year. There had been years with no rains even though the arrow had gone up into the sky. People then defended the belief by attributing the drought to prevalent injustice and bad dealings in the world. The priest would throw fruits from a basket towards the crowd after shooting the arrow. Whoever got the fruit considered himself to be blessed by the goddess. If it was a childless person who got the fruit, he would be blessed with a child.

One year there was a peculiar happening during the celebrations, and the thought of it never fails to amuse me.

One fellow, carrying his child on his shoulders, was trying to show him the goddess on the chariot pulled by the horses. The priest just then started throwing the fruits. Wanting to catch the fruit, the man put his child down. After getting the fruit, he was panic-stricken at not finding his child. He cried, 'Oh, my child, my child! Sankaiah, Sankaiah, please let me find my child. I will light a lamp made out of flour for you.' People were wondering why he would call out to a different god when it was the celebration for the Valmel Nadantha Amman. Then they came to know that Sankaiah was his family deity and he was from a place called Thiruvalloor.

In a little while there was an announcement in the loud speaker, 'A boy in black shorts and yellow shirt called Thangarasu, from Thiruvalloor, is here. Parents, kindly pick up the boy.'

Don't know if that fellow came alone or with his boy the next year. I wonder what decision he took.

After the celebrations, there would be karagattam. In those days, men would don the role of women. Pichamuthu Kumaran's troupe from Kalladithidal was the one I remember performing at this festival for many years. There were many among the nayandi drummers, who hailed from the north and south of my mother's birthplace – Keeranoor. None of them would reveal that they knew my parents. Even when they visited us the next day, they would have left behind their tharai, thapattai and kottumelam in some shop on the way. I would ask them about these and they would immediately say that they had sent them to their villages through somebody. After they went away my parents would say, 'They do not want anyone to know that they belong to the Parayar clan. So they come to see us without the instruments and go away immediately.'

Near Elayankudi High School there was a habitation called Rasoola Samudram. Only Parayars and Chakiliyars (Arundathiyar) lived here. There was a church, and it was a Lutheran church. Rasoola Samudram belonged to a Muslim from Pudur. He had given the place as a gift to the residents. I would hang out here during Christmas. Wilson was my friend, and it was he who taught me to play the harmonium. We used to sing during Christmas in the church, and on other days, in the scrub jungle near the market, unmindful of even the scorching sun. We sang songs like: *Enge Aval Manam*, *Ullam Enbadu Amai*, *Arupadai Veedu Konda Thirumuruga* and *Mullaimalar Mele*

There was Kalairaj Annan. He was from the Arundhathiyar caste. He was a friend of our machan, Dr Muniyandi. They used to put up plays for Christmas.

> What is the moon's anger against me
> It burns me like fire.

This was the duet for which Joseph and Virgin Mary would dance, which was followed by the nativity scene. Even now, during Christmas, these scenes come to my mind.

As I have often waited patiently to collect the sugar and dates that would be given during the celebrations at the Darga and after the fatiha is recited, I learnt a lot about Islamic rituals like the fatiha and namaz even at a very young age. Seeing me offering the prayers, Maimoon Periamma used to say, 'Gunasekara, you might as well convert to Islam.'

Within six or seven miles from Elayankudi there were many villages like Pavandan, Seethurini, Kalloorani, Valayanendhal, Karumbukuttam, Karunjuthi, Ariyanendhal, Ariyandapuram and Edayavalasai. When Father took me to see the plays put up at the annual temple celebrations in these places, I have experienced harassment in the name of caste and have often thought about converting to Islam. I have also seen the sunnath ritual many times in Elayankudi. I have been scared of becoming a Muslim after seeing sunnath being performed with a big knife to the accompaniment of recitals from the holy text, even as my friends on whom it was carried out let out cries due to unbearable pain.

In the Pavadi pond in Salaiyur, as well as in many other ponds in Elayankudi, there were separate places for women to bathe. There were raised walls, offering protection from intruding eyes. Young girls rarely come out of the house during day time. They would have their bath very early in the morning, even before dawn. I remember accompanying my mother and other young girls to the pond for a bath when I was still a small boy. Dragging me along in the dark, my mother would pacify my sleep-deprived, whimpering self by buying some appam for me to relish. As my mother was on the heavier side, the elders would tease her by calling her 'Gundalakesi'. The neighbours called her 'Mami', 'Chachi' or 'Machi' thereby establishing a closer relationship. They extended their friendship even after coming to know that we belonged to the Parayar caste, and this friendship continues till date.

We gave our friends nicknames, with adjectives prefixed to their names like 'Shit-rolling Jahangir', 'Butt-shaking Hamid' and 'Police dog Nasir'. Even when I addressed those older to me in familiar terms like 'Dei Mustafa', 'Come Sayyad' or 'What's up Kaja', it was never mistaken.

The clerk in the school in Elayankudi, where I studied classes six, seven and eight, was cross-eyed. He would enter the class with a list in his hand even while the classes were going on, and the class teachers did not mind this.

'How many in this class are Parayars?' he would ask. 'Put up your hands! How many are Pallars? Stand up, I will count. Look, all of you should come to the office after class to pick up your scholarship forms which should be filled up within a week's time and returned to the office.' Even now it hurts to think about those times when we had to stand up in front of the others in the class, shrinking and cringing. They would reinforce caste identities by labelling us Pallars, Parayars and Chakiliyars in front of our friends who never knew what caste was. Even then, Muslim boys had little awareness about Hindu caste divisions. And so I had no dearth of friends as long as I studied in Elayankudi up to the Pre-University class.

From second standard to SSLC I sang in the school prayer assembly. When Kamaraj, the Congress leader, visited Elayankudi, I sang, 'Ammavum Neeye, Appavum Neeye' a song from the film *Kalathoor Kannamma*, He appreciated my voice and the song of my choice by offering me the Kalimark colour-soda, which was served to him. From that day, till I finished school, I sang the prayer and the National Anthem at my school.

The prayer we sang up to fifth standard:

> *Bismillah Rahman Irrahim*
> God who rules us
> God who created us...

and, the songs we sang from sixth to eleventh standard, like:

> All glory to God
> Who created the world and
> Preserved it with unlimited Mercy

still echo in my memory.

During my High School days, our father enrolled my brother Karunanidhi and me in the Harijan Hostel for he could not afford our education. Attesting that Marandai was his birthplace, he got us enrolled at the Elayankudi hostel. I sang the prayer song of this hostel too, a famous film song that goes:

> Oh! Goddess who protects the justice
> Goddess who protects lineage…
> Oh! Parasakthi, give me the boon…

When we took our bath in the Muslim ponds we could not wear our loincloth alone. We had to wear a towel around the waist. One must not simply roam the market streets of Elayankudi. If we were asked about where we stayed, we were not to divulge information about the Harijan Hostel. Those who had itches and fungal infections should go to their houses until they were cured. These were some of the advices given to us unfailingly at the prayer assembly by our hostel leader.

> Nothing will ever change
> Neither rasam nor sundal

This was an amusing song sung by the warden. He would never distribute soap, oil and other things given to us by the government. Nor were we given anything other than buttermilk kanji, rasam and sundal to eat. Sambar and vegetables were never given to us. Food was never enough. Some of the well-to-do boys would eat the hostel food, and also eat poori masal at the Iyer hotel at Elayankudi on their way to school, and at night they would eat chappatis and a meat dish at the Muslim joint. We met to formulate a plan to stop the warden from committing this daylight robbery. One night we executed the plan.

It was decided that we would beat up this person who was responsible for our collective misery, after he doles out the ration for the next day. All of us knew the secret plan. One of us would switch off the light, one would close the door and four of us would take the cue and beat up the warden. Then when someone blew the whistle, someone would switch on the light and open the door… It was worse than what we had planned. The warden lost his teeth and was bleeding at the nose. He had a swollen face and was covered with blood.

The next day, the issue was brought to the attention of the thasildar. He decided to take action on a few and suspended them from the hostel for a month.

The Harijan Hostel was in Salaiyur. The High School was two kilometres away from there. One had to walk to the hostel for lunch and back to school again, a distance of about four kilometres. One had to accomplish this in one and half hours. All the hostel boys were used to walking fast for lunch. Small boys like me who could not cope with their speed would run behind them. Some would stay behind in school not wanting to walk four kilometres just to have lunch. 'Keep a plate for me' was what they would tell their friends everyday. The food would be left for them to be eaten in the evening after school. Even Muslim and poor high caste Hindus stayed in the hostel. Hostel boys, with a few exceptions, were generally good students.

We used to cook food together and make a game of it during the holidays. Picking up dry twigs and lighting the fire was a great task. Each would bring a tumbler of rice, and we would cook and eat it. I usually had to collect the dry twigs and fetch the water. We would take tips from Amsa Periamma the previous night itself for cooking our community lunch. Once, we had added a lot of salt and therefore had to pour a lot of water and drink it up. All the others in the group other than me were Muslims. We used to play kitti, pambaram, kilithattu and kabadi. Mother would scold me when I went back home dirty. Sometimes the scolding was supplemented by a wallop with a broomstick.

The people of Elayankudi were good football players. I have spent many hours watching people play the game, wearing vests of varying colours. Jamal was one of the good players (he is now a physical education instructor in Paris). When I was very young, on Id day, I have seen people donning themselves as a tiger and dancing. This practice died out later. At night, I used to listen to the stories told by Khadir. Stories of Nabi and Fathima were enthralling. Whatever the story narrated, the message stressed on being charitable, not taking dowry and the importance of praying five times a day – this being more essential than sleep.

There was a cinema tent called Green Talkies. Here, my mother used to sell tickets to the women. My friends and I would imagine ourselves as the hero, and riding our imaginary horses, would gallop towards the theatre, 'tok, tok, tok'. We did not buy tickets since Mother was employed at the theatre. Thus I came to see the same movie many times. The Jamaat had decided that Muslim women should not go to the cinema. Women who went despite this were fined. So at one point there were no women at the cinema and Mother lost her job.

During Ramzan, villages like Elayankudi, Salaipudur, Sothukudi and Mallipattinam would have a festive air about them. At the Hamidia School, where Father worked, and the Rahmania School, the bell would go at around 3 p.m. I would immediately rush home, leave my satchel and run to the mosque with a bowl. I would have the porridge given at the mosque, wash the bowl and get some more to be taken home. Many nights we would have no food at home. The porridge given at the mosque would serve as our dinner.

Our father had three sons and three daughters. My mother had been educated, even in those days, up to eighth standard at the Schwartz School in Ramanathapuram. In Keeranoor, where my mother was born, there was a church for Dalits. My mother was educated by the church authorities. Our father did not allow my mother to take up a government job. Looks like in those days there was not enough publicity for the Red Triangle. Having had half-a-dozen children, my father found it difficult to manage the house with his salary alone. Despite this, I came to know much later that he had another wife in Marandai with whom he had one son and two daughters. Our parents did not encourage all of us going out together, fearing the teasings of our neighbours. Nevertheless some Muslim neighbours would make fun of us as 'the staircase of the upper house' as we were born one after the other, with very little age gap. Often our father used to quarrel with Mother, mainly due to our poverty. Mother would then bundle her things and say, 'Come, let us go to my mother's place', and would make us walk to Keeranoor. After two or three days, Father would come and plead with Mother saying, 'The childrens' education is getting spoilt' and would take us back to our home.

Every year, when school re-opened, our father would ask some rich Muslims to help towards the cause of our education. They would buy us text-books and notebooks, and even paid our school fees. They would show respect to Father, even as they helped him. They would invite him into their homes saying, 'Come teacher, sit. Have some tea.' Our father too would please them with a salaam whenever he saw them.

I have already narrated the ordeal of getting the scholarship form at the school. To get the signature of the headman and the karnam was very difficult. If we go looking for him at Marandai, the karnam would be in Sethur. The headman in Sethur would all of a sudden adjourn to Elayankudi. It was difficult to even see them. If they saw us in the village they would ask us to tie up their cattle, dig out a canal, etc., and only then would they sign the forms. Father would feel frustrated every time he had to approach them for their signatures. 'It's horrid, the way they display their caste superiority before they sign anything', he would say.

To ease out the family problem, my elder brother Karunanidhi and I would angle for fish, during the quarterly and half-yearly leave. We would get enough fish near the women's ghat. My brother, being older, would teach me how to cast the line and would stand a little away from the place.

There used to be a protective wall around the place where the women took bath. Some women would shout at me for fishing in this spot. My elder brother would go to the other side to fish. If we went in the morning we would fish till evening, without even having our lunch. I would sell the fish on the streets of Elayankudi and Pudhur. I would bargain well, and took home anywhere between two to five rupees. We would buy rice with that money and have food for the night.

Sometimes a Muslim woman would be possessed by spirits. Rituals would be conducted to drive away these spirits. The paraphernalia used for such rituals would be thrown away on the banks of the ponds in the wee hours before dawn. My brother and I would go to such places and pick up the small coins that lay there and use it to buy peppermints and peanuts. We would not talk about it to Mother as she would scold us.

During the summer holidays, there would be no water in the ponds. Unable to fish, I would sell mangoes. The commission money given by the shop owner would be given to mother to buy rice. Mother, for her part, would cut the thorn trees for firewood, sell it to the Muslim neighbours and use the money to feed us. People who came to watch the first and second shows at the Green Talkies would leave their bullock-carts close-by. On some days, my mother would take me along to secretly collect the cow dung from this place. She would sell the flat dung-cakes, and use the money to support us. During the monsoon months she would cut grass and sell it to the Muslim houses. Most mornings we would only have soaked tamarind seeds for breakfast. The skin of the roasted seeds would be peeled off and the white kernel would then be soaked. If we had idlis or dosais, it ought to be either Deepavali or Christmas.

Due to poverty, our sisters, Kalavathi, Malathi and Jothi did not have the ear-piercing ceremony. One day my mother took my sister to the Saturday sandai, spent fifty paise to have her earlobes pierced and bought her a stud for one rupee. I feel sad when I think of how my sisters did not have a decent function for it like the others. Even today, when I look at the invitation for a puberty ceremony, I immediately feel the pang of pain that we couldn't afford such celebrations for my sisters.

We had always lived in a rented house. Very many times we had to shift because we could not pay the rent. Though I own my own house today, I cannot erase the memories of the bitter experiences at rented houses from my mind.

One such incident comes to mind. In fact, this place was not a house. It was meant to be a godown to stock things. It was big, with no walls inside to divide it. My youngest sister and brother were then over twelve years old. There was a lone palmyra tree in front of the house. The place was usually deserted at night and people avoided walking down that way. Behind the house there was a small unused pond. It had steps leading to it, and must have been in use a long time ago. The house and the grounds surrounding it belonged to a Muslim. Some days we would find some coins, cloth and rice placed under the palm tree indicating that the ritual for driving away the spirits of possessed women had taken place.

Though we were scared initially, we became used to it in due course. However, at night, if I were to go to the shops to get things, I would sing the song, 'Being scared is being stupid' and would summon all my courage to stand by me until I ran inside the house to safety. In case, even after singing this song, I was still nettled by fear, I would go back to Mariyam Biwi Periamma's house and would call out loudly for my mother. Mother would come with a lamp and take me home. As for me, after nightfall the lone palmyra that stood in front of the house was surely a devil. The eerie sound made by the palm leaves as they danced to the wind only increased my fear.

My friends had advised me to use chappal, broom or fire to make the spirits flee the place.

One day my sister Kala was possessed by a spirit. I caught her staring at me with her eyes open wide, and her eyeballs rolling up and down. Then she started laughing to herself and began wearing and and taking off our father's and brother's clothes. I was the only one at home then, and initially thought that she was joking. As time passed and she did not become normal, but continued doing all kinds of things, it occured to me that she was probably possessed. Escape was impossible, as Kala was seated by the doorway with her hair let loose and flying wild, and she would not move from there. Father had gone to Marandai and my elder brother was in Sivaganga College. My younger brother and Malathi had gone out just then for something. Mother had gone to Sambai to fetch some water from the pond. I thought about what to do. I tried calming her but she would not listen to me and was crooning to herself. I went closer. Near to where she was seated, next to the door, was a broom and a pair of slippers. I picked up both in a jiffy and showered blows on Kala. How I came out of that house is something which I have not understood till date. I had heard that beating with slippers and brooms will make the spirits leave the possessed body, so I tried this. Kala kept crying not able to bear the pain of the blows. She kept calling to Father and Mother for sometime and fell down like a log. After sometime I peeked in, and found her sleeping.

Mother came in just as it began to rain. Immediately we set about placing the vessels and gunny sack wherever the roof was leaking. Kala too joined me in this task. I told my mother then about what happened. That night, Mother took out her New Testament and asked Kala to keep it under her pillow. She also prayed that night, reciting 'Our father, thou art in Heaven', and she asked Kala to say 'Go away Devil'. From then onwards the spirit never came back to her. We all then sang, 'Praise to the Lord who was born in Bethlehem'.

Our parents told us to say that we were Christians if anyone asked us about our caste. They believed that Christians were not as obsessed with caste as the Hindus were.

In our family no one had gone even once to the Rasoola Samudram Church. I was the only one who went to sing the Christmas and New Year carols along with my friend Wilson. It was then that I wrote songs about Christ and set them to cinema song tunes to be sung at the church. A Muslim friend played the drums, and Hussain Bai, the tea master, sang the songs. Our troupe has sung at the Vazhividu Pillayar Koil for just a coconut.

In the Muslim households men were by and large in foreign countries. We were paid to read out their letters. We also wrote to the husbands entreating them to send money for their children. We were paid up to three rupees for these services. Muslim girls would weave mats out of kora grass in their Salaiyur houses. If we took them to Moolthadiyan shop or to N.H. Jalal and sold them, we would be given money. Sometimes we would read aloud books on the life of Nabi, and they would listen as they weaved their mats. They would pay us for this and also give us money to buy more books. 'Gunasekara, go and see this movie and come back and tell me the story', would also be a request from them. They would give me money for narrating the plotline and singing the cinema songs, and they would exclaim, 'Listening to you, we didn't realise time passing as we were weaving. Here, go and eat panniyaram and drink tea at Chekkadiyatan tea shop and get some for us too.'

In my young age, when I told cinema stories, I could see that the ladies preferred MGR, while I liked Sivaji. If on my way to school, I hear some popular song being broadcast on the radio, I would stop and listen, and would move only after it ended.

From the money that I got by selling neem seeds to Moolthadiyan shop, I would hire a bicycle to learn cycling. I would go to Paramakudi by cycle. On the way there is a place called Kumarakurichi. My friends Kaja, Jehangir, Mustafa and I would be scared of crossing this place, as the residents of Kumarakurichi had a terrible reputation. They were capable of even stopping the buses which ply via their village. Since we had heard much about them we felt relieved only after we crossed this village.

In school, every year we had a sports meet. Winners of fancy-dress, singing and oratorical contests, and also essay-writing competition, were given prizes only on that day. I would participate in almost all the competitions and win some prize or the other. I used to come first in 100 m and 200 m relay races. Instructed by my elder brother Karunanidhi, I used to train a week ahead of the sports day by walking on my toes. Only then, during the race the legs would sprint like a spring. My anna and Muniyandi Machan studied in my school before me and they too were excellent in sports and had won the Championship Cup too. There used to be a 1000 m running race for the public to participate in. Many elders used to participate in it. Usually a person belonging to Keezhayur would definitely be there. He would be the only one who was ebony dark among the fair-skinned Muslims. While the others ran the first four rounds steadily and would aim at finishing ahead of others in the fifth round, the Keezhayur man would run fast from the beginning and finish the race first. When he was called to receive the prize, they referred to him as the Keezhayur man.

When I was studying SSLC in Elayankudi, the Jamaat decided to build a college and started collecting donations to that end. Cultural programmes were also conducted to collect donation. Khader Kani Sir was then the Tamil teacher. He prepared a play called *Theeran Tippu Sultan*, and Shahjahan Kani Sir prepared the sets, including a crouching tiger made of paper mould, painted to look like a real one. I was the lead singer of this play. Since I was busy playing an important role in the play that was going to help in the founding of the Elayankudi college, I failed in Mathematics in the SSLC exam. I was allowed to continue with my studies in the High School during the second year, even though this was never done before.

I mentioned a person who was very good in football, didn't I? He was Paris Jamal. He asked Father one day, 'Sir, Gunasekaran sings very well. Our Elayankudi Government hospital nurse's son is cinema director Mahendran. If we approach him, Gunasekaran will become famous in cinema. Shall I do it?' Father was also interested, but his sister's son Muniyandi was studying medicine. He was educated by my father and Chithappa since his early school days. Muniyandi Machan said, 'No Mama, Gunasekaran should study.' It was because of him that I continued my studies.

I once again failed in mathematics. I decided to take the exam again in October. N.H. Jalal who had a mat shop in Salaiyur had worked hard to have a shop in Sothukudi. I found employment in his shop. When he worked in the ration shop, I had assisted him. I would prepare bills, weigh sugar in the balance, etc. The scales that I used to weigh the sugar would be lined with paper. People never suspected anything. Easily 100 g of sugar would be less in every kilo – Jalal would have so many layers of papers lining the scales.

He would take me to his house once in a while. He had a big, palatial house. But, he had two elder brothers who were not mentally sound. They would always be seated on the thinnai outside the house. No one came forward to give their girls in marriage to them. Even Jalal did not think about marriage as he felt he too might lose his mind someday. But he used to speak at length about the then actors and actresses. Since I was a good friend of his, he employed me in his shop. Every afternoon we would eat tasty food that came from his house.

The distance between Elayankudi and Sothukudi would be around four kilometres. I would cover this distance by cycle every morning, with Jalal riding pillion behind me. In the evening, likewise, I would drop him home. As I pedaled furiously across this distance, I would be oppressed by an anger at failing and inflamed by a desire to study. One night, as we were returning home, I hit against a milestone on the road – this road ran close to the irrigation canal. Jalal fell into this canal. Later, this was a story he enjoyed narrating to people. It was because of his help that I paid the fees, went to Ramanathapuram and cleared all nine papers in the secretarial course in one attempt. In those days unless one passed all the nine papers in a single attempt one could not join college. I wrote the exam in Syed Mohammed Ammal School by taking the typewriter from my village in a hired horse carriage. I was the only one to pass the secretarial course in October in the entire Ramanathapuram district. I worked the whole year in Jalal's shop, and with this earnings studied PUC.

I joined PUC in Dr Zakir Hussain College which was founded

with the donation collected by staging plays. I stood first in most of the inter-college singing and acting competitions. I made a mark for myself in the college and can never forget Shahjahan Kani Sir, who taught me to act.

'Even if he were to eat plate after plate, he would ask for more and more – this blackguard.' – This dialogue, written by him, and spoken by me in the play *Election in the Heavens* can never be forgotten.

There were a few Harijan students like Arulandu and Samidoss. There would be no food for those who did not pay the mess fees at the hostel. My father would get the help of the Jamaat and would somehow pay my fees. I would hide idli, dosai, uthappam, etc., from the mess, in the kaili that I wore, and would bring it to my friends who were denied food at the hostel. I would also pack my lunch and share it with them. And so, the Harijan students were very fond of me, and so were my teachers. The Harijan students would use my name to become friends with other students and teachers.

Pavadi was a beautiful place in Salaiyur. There used to be a well, pump set and a big tank where water would get accumulated. One could always see some Muslim having his bath over there. There were many canals carrying water, a coconut grove and a big naaval tree in this spot. Near these were some old trees like Pongamia, banyan, tamarind, etc. Altogether a cool place. The pond nearby had a high bund around it. We would climb on to the bund and trees to jump into the water and would swim for hours.

Fridays were holidays at the Hamidia School where I studied. There were two tamarind trees in the school. We used to play football in the ground adjacent to them, dividing ourselves into two groups – one group under the captainship of Pushparaj headmaster and the other under some other master. We used to play from 4 to 4.30 p.m. on all days when there were no rains. Selvaraj teacher was in-charge of drama and singing. My father, Azhagan teacher, was in-charge of speeches. David teacher took care of discipline and lining up the boys. Amanulla teacher was in-charge of cooking and made excellent uppuma for lunch.

One day, an unfortunate kasukatti bird came into the classroom. Its bottom was red in colour. Amanulla sir said, 'Dei, boys, close all the windows.' The moment he asked us to close the windows we left our lessons and did so. He wound a cloth around a duster and threw it at the bird and asked the boys to roll their shirts and throw at the bird. All of them did so and the poor bird after some time, unable to cope with the attack, fell down. Sir took it to the kitchen and when he came back after some time, the boys asked him, 'Sir, Have you finished eating it? How was it?', and he replied, 'It was very nice. Turn to your lessons now.' I felt very heavy the whole day thinking of the pretty Kasukatti bird being attacked by rolled-up shirts.

During the rainy season, Amanulla Khan Sir would ask us to read our books, and would keep humming cinema songs loudly.

> Cold wind, Oh cold wind
> Why do you scorch my youthful heart?

This song that he hummed remains fresh in my memory even now.

My father, Azhagan Teacher, used to tell the stories of Kannagi, Ramayanam and Mahabharatham in a very interesting manner. 'You should learn by rote the two to nine tables and must write them out tomorrow. Gunasekara, if you do not do so, I will make you vomit all the milk that you had from your mother.' He would threaten me so in front of all the boys. The boys would be scared, since the teacher was harsh with his own son. So they would study well. The days I did not receive beatings were rare.

In those days, boys who did not come to school were made to wear a wooden block tied to a chain around their leg. They had to carry it around school. After school hours the key would be sent to their homes. Anyone who underwent this punishment would never dream of abstaining from the classes.

One day, it was almost time for the recess bell. Two fellows who had stolen sugarcane from Chinnathambi Ambalakarar's fields were caught and were marched on the streets with their hands tied and with not a stitch on them. The bell did not go since the teachers did not want us to see the parade. Even so, some of us, fourth standard boys, climbed the window to catch the spectacle. Chinnathambi Ambalakarar's groves were behind our school and he was well known in Elayankudi and around. In a place largely dominated by the Konars and Thevars this gentleman's bravado made his people proclaim, 'It is because there is a Muslim like him that the other Muslims are able to live in peace.'

Whether we carried our books or not in our satchel, when we were studying in Hamidia School our bags had either a dung cake or firewood. Unless we gave these, we were not given our noon meal. Most of the boys who had this noon meal were Dalit boys in and around Elayankudi. My father, Selvaraj Sir, Davis Teacher, and another teacher whose real name I do not know even today were all Dalit teachers. A teacher whose name I do not remember had the habit of folding his full sleeve before he gave a knock on the head of the boy who had committed a wrong. The knock would be accompanied by a swear word; and the boys started referring to him by that swear word.

Mallipattinam was only a kilometre away from Salaiyur. On the banks of the Pavandan canal, the Malllipattinam Muslim darga had been constructed. Once a year the Kandoori celebrations would take place over here. They would then play various instruments like kombu, tharai, thapattai, thavil, pambai, etc. and most of those who played these instruments came from our mother's place. Most of them were also our relatives.

Some friends and I were returning to the hostel one night from the Pavandan canal. Near the Mallipattinam darga, an electric wire had fallen off the pole onto the road. As it had rained, there were puddles on the road and the live wire proved dangerous. A poor fellow, unaware of this, was electrocuted and he now lay dead on the road, with his hand across his chest. A Gurkha standing on the other side warned us of the danger and asked us not to proceed further. Having taken one look at the dead body by the light of a torch, we ran back to the darga. Next day we came to know that the dead 'man' was our classmate. That day was declared a holiday by the school. Ever since that day I have kept away from electricity.

2

My brother and I would go to my periamma's house for the quarterly, half-yearly and annual vacations. Thovoor is less than six miles from Elayankudi. In those days there were no buses. One had to walk the entire stretch. If we start from Salaiyur in the morning we would reach Thovoor in the evening.

The moment we reached Kaloorani the smell of sweet palm wine would waft in the air. The air was redolent with the heady scent of the making of palm sugar. We would stop near the Saanar settlements and ask them for pathaneer. For five or ten paise we would get pathaneer in a bowl made out of palm leaves. Whichever village we entered, the first question would be 'Who are you?', and the moment they knew we were Parayars, they would not offer us a drink in a vessel, but would pour it only in the folded palm leaf. We would walk after having fortified ourselves with the pathaneer. We would find ourselves thirsty by the time we reached Karunchutti. Even before they gave us water, the question, 'Who are you?' would be asked. There were about fifty Muslim families and a mosque in Karunchutti. Even if we asked a Muslim household for water, they too would ask us, 'Who are you?' before they offered us water. In Elayankudi and Salaiyur one was never asked this question. I asked my brother Karunanidhi, 'Why is it that the Muslims in this village alone ask about our caste and then make us drink water with our cupped hands?' He said, 'The Muslims here are surrounded by many other castes like Saanar, Konar, etc. They must have learnt from them. That is why these people are also aware of caste.'

While walking down the road we would see sugarcane fields

on either side. Feeling thirsty we would crouch near the Thovoor canal and drink water by scouring it with both hands. We would be very, very careful about not disturbing the water. Otherwise the water would become muddy and smelly. We did not know to which caste this canal belonged. 'If it belongs to the upper caste we would be tied to a tree and beaten. So run', we would say to each other and take to our heels. Even sedately running water would intimidate us, in the name of caste, in the villages surrounding Elayankudi.

One day when we were walking towards Thovoor, there was a bullock cart going ahead of us without any load. My brother was walking ahead of me. I asked the cartman if I could get on to the cart. The cartman asked me, as he continued to drive, 'What kind of a fellow are you?'

Thinking that he was not able to make out if I was a boy or a girl, I answered, 'I am a boy.'

'No, no, I am asking your varnashramam?'

'I will ask my brother who is going ahead there,' I said, and ran to ask my brother, overtaking a cat, 'What is varnashramam?'

My brother said, 'We are Parayars. I knew that fellow would ask our caste and that is why I did not ask him for a ride in his cart. Don't get on the cart. Do you see, there in the distance is our periamma's village. Come, let us walk.'

The cart just then caught up with us. The cartman asked, 'Dei, what is your caste?'

'Parayar', I said.

'Get on the cart,' he said.

My brother and I replied in chorus, 'No need.'

The cartman asked, 'So, who are you visiting?'

'We are going to John's house. His son's name in Arpudam and that is our periamma's house', I said.

We reached the cheri via the canal whose banks had tamarind trees. There is a church in Thovoor for the cheri people. The preacher or the priest would come from Kilanchunai, either on a cycle or a motor bike. They would come only on Sunday mornings.

On Christmas day they would be there both in the morning and evening.

Grace, Kunjaram and Kuzhandayamma of Thovoor were my friends. My annan had Balu, Maduraiveeran, Chinnathangarasu and Periyathangarasu as his friends. My periamma would send me to collect dry sticks in the mornings, and in the evenings she would send me to grind the grain.

The people of Thovoor were fascinated by our clothes. They felt that we were very fashionable because we came from a town. How would they ever know what our life was like in the town? After all they were only looking at our external appearance.

Some of my father's students who had been to Malaysia and Singapore gave us three or four shirts or t-shirts as gifts. I do not remember my father wearing any of those. He would sell what was given to him as gift for fifteen rupees or so in Pullappan's shop. He would use that money to buy rice and pulses for the house. We used to buy old shirts and pants for four to ten rupees from that same Pullappan's shop. We would alter them to size before we wore them. I don't remember my father ever buying new clothes for us. We have never bought fish as I have seen Muslims buy them. Father would buy only what was left behind. 'Azhagan teacher has lots of children. Collect all that is remaining and give it to him', the fish shop owners would tell their assistants. Even in the mutton shop the same story got repeated. We were eight of us – father, mother and half a dozen children. There was always a shroud of privation around us.

In spite of this situation, there was not a single day when the house did not have a visitor from the village. Father and Mother never sent away anyone without making them sit down for at least one meal. Only we children would be worried about losing out from our share of the food. Even when we ate in the hostel, some nights, Ismail and I would go to my house to eat at least a little bit. It was my father who brought him from Sothukudi and put him in Elayankudi High School and in the Harijan Hostel. Till he joined the hostel, Ismail stayed in our house and ate with us. He is like a brother to us; Ismail is at present a teacher in the Parthibanoor Higher Secondary School.

Father would function as a scribe for the people who came from the villages to give a petition to the police, the hospitals and the tahsildar's office. He would accept the tea, sweetmeats and bread that these people brought for him, and would rarely eat at home. How would the Thovoor people know that our lives were in such a condition at Elayankudi?

Kunjaram, Kuzhandayamma, Grace and others in Thovoor who took me with them to collect firewood were older to me by a few years. The moment we entered the scrub jungle they would spot the shade of a big tree and say, 'Sit here. If you come along and chop the thorny wood the sickle or thorn might hurt you: you may bleed. You just sit here and keep singing. We will chop wood for you; we'll give you your bundle when we get to your periamma's place.' I too would happily sit singing cinema songs. Sometimes I would also narrate cinema stories. 'Gunasekara, why don't you join the cinema?' they would ask me. And I would tell them, 'I need to study, and after I grow up I would join the cinema.'

Early in the morning, even before the orange ball of sun came up, Kunjaram and the others would wake me up by calling out, 'Gunasekara, come, let us go to the Chinna Thovoor ayya's land and pick pulses.' We used to pick the pulses as fast as possible. The pulses would in fact come out with roots, shoots, etc., into my basket. While the others filled four baskets I would have filed only two. If we fill four baskets, the owner would keep three and we would get one.

Some days we would take paddy in a basket, grind it, give the husk as the payment and bring the rice home. Carrying paddy in a basket was an onerous task. Our neck would pain and we would be immensely thirsty. We would go to Iyyampatti, about three miles from Thovoor, to grind paddy. The basket would weigh less on our return journey as the paddy would have been dehusked.

During the annual vacation, Anna and I would go to Thovoor. On these days, as soon as it became dark we would enact a few plays. My anna, Maduraiveeran, Balu, Minardas and others used to take part – very often it would be the play called 'Samrat Asokan'. People enjoyed the performance. They used to say, 'The Elayankudi fellows have come and they would put up plays at night.' After the show, we would spread out hay and sleep on the stack. At dawn, even before one was properly awake, one heard shouts from various directions asking people to come to work: 'Ei, Arulayee, Annapushpam, Muniya, will four of you come to pick chilies? I had asked for ten of you to cut the corn yesterday itself. Come, it's already late. Come quickly. What happened? I asked Siluvaimuthu to make a winnow. Has he finished doing it? We need it tomorrow to winnow the grains in the field.' ..... 'Ei, Thangarasu, will you come to divert the water into the fields? Come, get the oxen for ploughing... Two more people are needed to make the bund'. We used to sleep till the sun literally scorched us – we were tired after having put up our late night show. By noon, only those fellows with no work would remain in the cheri. Only after those who went about their various jobs in the day came back would the cheri once again buzz with activity. My periamma's son, Arpudam Anna, never sang more than a couple of lines of any cinema song. But his voice could be heard even as far away as the well from which people fetched water.

Arpudam Anna, Thangarasu and Tamilarasi Akka were studying in Thovoor school. Arpudam Anna secured the first prize in running race on Sports Days. One night Anna confessed that he had drunk two big glasses of toddy that Periamma had bought. His teachers and the other boys were ignorant of this fact. He got the prize only because he had drunk the toddy. Even today I am perturbed by the fact that this happened in an educational institution.

Once I had set up a shop with a gift sheet in front of Arpudam Anna's school. I had bought it from Maimoon Periamma's wholesale shop to sell it to the Thovoor school boys. The sheets came to Salaiyur from Madurai. Before I tell you about the incident that happened there shall I tell you what a gift sheet is? The sheet has the numbers 1 to 100, and the numbers would be covered with another paper. With four annas or ten paise we would be given the chance to scratch open a particular spot. Supposing there was a number underneath and that number had a particular object as a gift then one can claim it. Bowls, money, pencils, purses, erasers, pictures and balls were some of the gift items. A person can scratch as many spots as he has paid for. If lucky he would get a gift. If unlucky there would be no number.

I set up the shop anticipating the recess time for the boys. The boys came running the moment the bell rang. Since this lottery was new to them the business picked up quickly. One fellow gave fifty paise and scratched out five spots. Not even one had a number. So I told him, 'That's it. If you want to scratch some more, you need to give me more money.' Promising to give money, he kept on tearing. He scratched upto fifteen spots. Whenever there was a number he had a gift item like eraser, ball, clock, etc. Before I gave the gift items to him, I demanded the money that he owed me. He said he had no money.

'Why did you scratch without money,' I asked.

He replied haughtily, 'What else can I do when I don't have money?'

'Ei, do you know that my Arpudam anna studies here?' I asked.

The fellow answered, 'Is Arulai's son Arpudam, your brother?' I said, 'Yes.'

'Do what you want. I can't give you the money', he said.

I caught hold of his shirt. He didn't expect it. The bell rang. All the other boys ran into the school. I held on to his shirt and didn't let it go. Even before I could finish telling him, 'If you go to school without giving me the money I will tell your teacher,' he got rid of my hold and ran away saying, 'Get lost, Paraya.' I chased after him. Maybe he thought, 'I belong to the Konar caste. If I go to our street and into my house he will not follow me.' His conjecture was wrong. I was an Elayankudi fellow. I have never bothered with the segregation of certain castes in the villages. I chased him, and he ran through the streets and at last he hid inside his house. I too went inside his house and searched for him. Just behind the granary I heard him breathing hard. I pulled him by the hair and gave a few blows. The fellow yelled in pain and called out to his parents. I knew his folks would come hearing his cries. I took to my heels and stopped only after reaching the school. I took the lottery sheet and went to the cheri.

That night at around 8 o'clock, about eight men came with that boy to my periamma's house. I was just then having my dinner. The moment I heard their voices outside, I went and hid myself. It was a thatched house. Even if they came in, they wouldn't have been able to spot me in the darkness. On the thinnai outside, my periamma and periappa fell at their feet and propitiated them, 'Ayya, he is my younger sister's son and is brought up in a town. He does not know anything about our village ways.' The men kept asking, 'How can a fellow from your caste enter the upper caste street? And worse, how dare he enter our house.'

'If the fellow had entered our house without knowing the limitations of his caste, then he must really be very arrogant. Where is he? Let's tie up his feet and hands, and carry him away', they shouted.

I was panic-stricken.

The people of the cheri had also assembled outside the house. The crowd finally dispersed after some time. Nobody talked about the boy who was beaten. They were only worried about a Paraya entering their street and their house, not caring for the rigidity of caste. The moment they went away the people in my periamma's house said, 'We should send him away to Elayankudi first thing in the morning.' And true to their words, I was sent away with my periamma the next morning. Both of us had bundles of paddy, rice and chilies on our head and as we were walking my periamma kept cursing, 'Casteless fellows, fellows belonging to bad caste, ...'

'From the day I came to Thovoor, after my marriage, I have never worn a blouse. The cheri women were not allowed to wear blouses as per the caste regulations of the village. Girls my age who came to this village after their marriage too have been subjected to this practice, and have not worn a blouse to this day.' Talking about these matters my periamma and I walked back to Elayankudi. It was my mother who thrashed me with the broom saying, 'Not capable of behaving yourself wherever you go, is it? Useless fellow.'

Once our periamma took us to watch the Kazhugadiyan temple festival at Thovoor. The place merely had a sharp rod like structure, almost like the tool we use to dehusk a coconut, and they called it a temple. In the midst of the fields there was a slightly elevated place, where the cocks were killed and offered to the deities along with gruel. The place now has an iron fence around it. On festival days, folk-plays would be enacted through the night. Everyone in the village would come to watch. The stage used to be put up in the middle of the fields. Only the sick and immobile would be left behind in the village. In order to prevent thieves from entering the village, the villagers would elect a few to be appointed as watchmen. My periappa was always a part of this team. He was strong, tall and muscular, and was called 'Mota'. At the place where the performances were staged there used to be a rope segregating the men and women.

Over the mike the announcement would often be made entreating the men not to go to the side reserved for women. The women could sit with whomever they pleased. Maduraiveeran and Balu told me it was so.

Both men and women would bow and pay their respects to the iron rod-like things on the sand mound in the Kazhugadiyan temple, and then go to their fields. No one would go near this temple at night, as the deities were supposed to be rather violent. Women, in particular, would never go anywhere near this temple at night. When I read about the Jains being quartered by the Saivites while studying for my M.A in Tamil, I linked the place of punishment with this temple.

Anna and I used to be in Thovoor during the Pongal festival. It was only in my Arulai periamma's house that we ever had full meals. The people belonging to the Thovoor cheri would never sleep much of the nights, even a month before the harvest festival. Men would weave winnows and women would make boxes of all kinds and shapes with the palmyra leaves. All these people would say that they were making boxes for their parent's house or mats for their relatives' houses. On the harvest festival day they would take all that they had been making for over a month – mats, winnows, boxes, baskets, etc., to the land owners' houses. In return they would be given money, new vettis, sarees, towels, etc., along with the new rice that would have been cooked that day.

In the cheri every Paraya house and the Chakiliyar house, would have an upper-caste master. There would be no day when they would not talk about 'our master's house'. When I think about it now I feel it was a kind of slavishness. My periamma would give me mats and new boxes, along with one old box and tell me, 'On the banks of the canal, is our master's house amidst the tamarind trees... Just go and stand there. If they ask you who you are, just tell them that you are Arulai's younger sister's son. They would give you newly cooked rice in the old box. Take it and give them these new mats and boxes.' I would do as she said and on the way back pick out the cashews, raisins, etc., in the sweet rice in the box. Then I would start eating the rice little by little till I reached home. The mats, winnows and boxes that are made by these people would be used by their masters. When I think of this now, I understand it to be a kind of exploitation by the upper caste people.

The youngsters in Thovoor would join together and fish at the canals, fields and places where water used to stagnate. They would devise ways of drying them up in order to collect the fish that would be lying at the bottom. We used to get a variety of fresh water fish – delicacies which we haven't seen for a long time since.

Announcing deaths used to be referred to as 'carrying "news" to the villages'.

The keening began with, 'Hey you guys! Haven't you taken the news to the villages?' If anyone died in the upper caste households, the local people from the cheri will have to carry the news to their relatives in other villages. The messenger was not paid for this service. But the person receiving the news would give a measure or two of paddy, and that was accepted as wages.

Many people from the cheri would set out in different directions by walk carrying the news. They had to reach various places on the same day; it was imperative that the news of grief should reach all to ensure their presence at the funeral. In those days there was no bus facility and one had to walk.

I have also gone with Maduraiveeran and Balu carrying news from the grief stricken households to places which were within eight kilometre distance like, Viradhakandan, Sokkapaddappu, Anandur, Vadathirukai, Alavidanga, etc. We would sell the paddy given to us in these villages at the small shops in the same place, and buy all kinds of things to eat. The money that is left over would often be used to watch a movie at Salaigramam, Paramakudi and Anandur. We were quite adept at delivering this death news to the relatives. We would announce, 'So and so in Thovoor has passed away and the funeral will be at the early hours the next day.' The moment such news was conveyed the woman folk would start lamenting and crying. We would declare that we were on our way to the next village, and they would give us the paddy. We would hold out our towels and they would tip the measure of grain into it. Depending on the closeness of the relationship with the dead, the number of measures of paddy would increase or decrease.

Some houses would offer us rice, porridge or gruel. If anyone invites us to eat we would first ask for a sickle to cut the palmyra leaf and make a bowl for ourselves. Not a drop would leak from Maduraiveeran's bowl. I got an opportunity to travel to many places and visit many villages while carrying the news about the death. We would pick up tender palmyra fruits, cucumbers, brinjals, palm fruits, etc., as we walked from place to place. Then only would we proceed to those houses where we had to deliver the news.

On the way we would talk about the problems that our grandfathers and great-grandfathers had to face because of their caste. There was a time when we carried such news as it fetched good money for us. Minardas was of our age, and he used to draw very well. He was the one who used to make fun of us saying, 'One can die pulling out one's tongue instead of going from place to place carrying news of grief, to earn money for eating and seeing movies.' Minardas was a boy who fought with that village leader. Disgusted with the affairs of the village he ran away to Bombay. After ten or fifteen years of stay there, he went to London. At present he is in Sivaganga with his children having built a house there.

Every year in the month of Masi, there would be a cattle chase in the Muniayya temple. The Thovoor people to this day reiterate that there has never been such a bad event as it was that particular year. Muniayya temple lies at the corner of the road, between Thovoor and Salaigramam, on the way to the sugarcane fields. Popular belief has it that people would vomit blood if Muniayya showered blows on them. Always the female deities and other deities within the village would be very calm and gentle. But Sankaiah, Kazhugadiyan and Muniayya, the male deities who stay outside the village, are perceived as being hot tempered.

A form of bull fighting is seen in many villages. The cattle in the village would be made to become violent by loud drumming and by chasing them around. The bulls which ran down the track would have towels, vettis, money bags, sugarcane or tubers tied around their necks. The person who controls the bull would get the bounty around its neck. If a group of men succeed in restraining it, they would share the prize among themselves. The bulls which participate in such contests are selected for their ferocity. They would be chased through a narrow gully and people would attempt to control them.

I have seen big bulls taking part in such contests in Thiruvallur, Keerikudi, Pudhur and Pavandan villages. A thick rope would be tied around the bull's neck. The rope would be forty or fifty feet long. As the bull races past, people who intend to control it would try to pull the rope. The trained bull would charge against all those who attempt to tease it by pulling the rope. The men would then run away helter-skelter. Then the bull would run towards its owner – the village heads would decide where he is supposed to be stationed. If it manages to run around four or five times without getting caught, then the owner would be given four or five thousand thousand rupees as prize money. In case the bull is subdued, then the person who achieved this feat is given the money. Men, women and children crowd around the place where the bulls run. They would stand on the fields and bunds to watch the event. Generally youngsters take part in the event. Of course, parents of young women of marriageable age scout these contests to assess the prowess of the youngsters. People from various other villages would also assemble. That night there would be plays put up by the drama troupe of Sankaradas Swamigal.

Let us see what happened in the cattle chase at the Muniayya temple. Since the people generally believed that by making their bulls participate in the Muniayya temple contest they would be blessed with good health, there used to be many participants in this race. Only two or three of the bulls would have firm backs and be good runners. They would get angered and agitated by the noise made by the people around. Some will be so scared that they will not stand still. The bulls which escape the crowd would run helter-skelter and enter other villages. People would search for them for the next few days. Getting to know of their whereabouts they would go to the palmyra groves or thorn fields to bring them back. Many would therefore hesitate to take part in this contest.

That particular year there were plenty of bulls and there was a big crowd. The fields were teeming with men. One of the bulls suddenly charged into the crowds. The screams and shouts of the people made it all the more agitated, and it started kicking and butting all those who were around. The village heads, who arranged for the contest, too were stunned by this incident.

Around ten to twenty people were hurt and bleeding. Only after having wreaked havoc did the bull swim through the canal water and go to the other side. The relatives of those who were hurt took them to the doctor. Muniya's sister, it was told, was hurt by the horns of the bull tearing her stomach. We found her in a pool of blood.

There were only two Chakiliyar houses in the village. They and the Parayas got along fine. It was these Chakiliyars who took Muniya's sister from where she had fallen, helped her gain consciousness and dressed her gored stomach with a wet saree. They took her in a bullock cart to the hospital at Elayankudi. They kept her there for a day and then moved her to a hospital in Madurai. My machan's classmate gave a letter of recommendation to Madurai hospital. I was then doing my M.A. in Madurai Thyagaraja College. I would visit her everyday at the hospital. She had her husband and daughter Kunjaram helping her. She seemed happy. I would give her money to buy food whenever I visited her. After four or five days she died. We didn't expect it. I still believe it was because of the indifference of the government doctors that she died: if they had been attentive her stomach could have been stitched up and she could have been saved. If we had had money we would have admitted her in a private hospital. I had thought she would survive. My machan and Kunjaram kept crying. There was no money and no facility to take her back to Thovoor. Everytime I've visited Thovoor I have always been given a meal in her house. A person who cared so much for me, like a mother, was lying in the hospital, dead and alone. Thinking of this I wept copious tears. At last we hired a hand cart and took her body to Madurai Tattaneri funeral ground. We had no relatives or our caste people around. My machan, his daughter and my thambi Sathyabalan walked behind me. We went to the funeral ground, paid money, and buried her. A Paraya who lived around those parts, heard of our sad state and helped us bury her. When I went back to Thovoor along with my machan and his daughter, the entire village stood around weeping for her. The land owners too came to offer the grieved family their consolation. It was Muniya's sister who gave medical advice to the villagers who suffered from casual ailments. The lady who helped very many people wasn't alive anymore. One day I had had stomach ache. Muniya's sister came to see me as I was rolling on the floor with pain, made me stand with my hands raised above my head, and tapped my stomach with her fingers. When she heard a hollow sound she said it was due to flatulance and asked me to grind drumstick leaves and take it with water. In a short while my discomfort and pain were gone. I was upset that the person who had helped so many had such an unfair end. My travels to Thovoor was also coming to an end.

One night, my periamma at Thovoor was bitten by a snake. A cart was borrowed from the land owner to take her to Elayankudi. We got the news later that she had died on the way. My annan Karunanidhi was holding a government job in Mandapam. He hastened from there. I came from Sivaganga to Thovoor. My mother hugged my periamma's mortal remains and cried, 'How will I save my children? How could the snake bite the leg that brought rice, paddy and maize for us? How could the snake bite the hands that brought up my children?' We too on our part lamented calling out to our dead aunt. Periappa broke down crying, 'Oh my peacock! My peacock! Where did you go away? Where have you gone leaving me alone?' My periamma's only son, Arpudam, could not come immediately from Bombay. He came after a week, lay down on the grave and wept calling out to her. The Arulai periamma who sat under that neem tree calling out to us, 'Dei Gunasekara, Karunanidhi…', and who fed us, was no more. My annan Arpudam's wife, Annapushpam Athachi is much attached to us, and shows us affection as my periamma used to do.

3

My mother's younger sister, Thavamani, would often come to Thovoor from my birthplace, Marandai. Before Deepavali the schools would close for quarterly holidays. I would go to Thovoor during these holidays. One day my cinamma took me to clear out what we call 'morning weeds'. We would set out before dawn and finish by eight in the morning. I would quietly work next to her. The younger ones would get four annas and the elders would get two rupees. Since I was brought up in the Muslim town of Elayankudi, I never knew the difference between paddy saplings and weeds. Every now and then I would cut out the paddy saplings and cover them up with mud. Sometimes my cinamma would help me weed out the portion that was allocated to me. One day I picked up a four anna bit in the field, 'I've got today's earnings. I have found four annas', I yelled at the top of my voice, threw down the hoe, and ran from the field hoping to escape the labour that day. 'Dei, if you weed out for a little more time, you would get another four annas. Come boy, come', said my cinamma and made me complete the work. I had thus earned around twelve rupees. When I went back to Elayankudi, my mother took the money away from me to buy rice. I gave it to her because she promised to get me new clothes for Deepavali. Generally we would only buy second-hand clothes from Pullappan's shop for this festival.

It was only when I went to the temple festivals at Thovoor, that I saw the street plays, the Koravan-Kurathi dances and karagattam. I also listened to many songs like:

> In the Saturday sandai, Shymala – for you

> I will get sweet Pongal, Shymala!
> In the Sunday sandai, Shymala – for you
> I will get a G-string, Shymala!

Another popular song was:

> The thorn of the Karuvellam pierces me – hey girl
> Hurting both my feet!

Azhagarsami Teacher of Salaigramam, known to everyone as Pacheri Azhagan, and his disciples would perform the karagam and Kurathi dances. I used to fiddle around with their instruments like pambai, urumi and thavil. Most of the dancers and musicians from the Thovoor cheri would be related to these people. They would leave their drums tied to the trees around the cheri. They would never say anything if I tried to play on them. Most of the performers would advertise themselves as people from Kalladithidal, Yerivayal, Sooranam, Salaigramam, Rasiamangalam, Puliadithamam, Uridikottai, Paramakudi, Emaneswaram, Ramanathapuram, Keeranoor, Pudukottai and Thanjavur. Even if they are from Pudukottai and Thanjavur they are basically from places in and around Thovoor and settled in these far away towns for the sake of their profession. They had gone out of their hometowns mainly to escape the oppression of the upper caste. If they had stayed on they would have had to do as they were bidden. And their artistry would be written off as service to the village. It was generally slavish work without recompense. That is why these artists went away to distant places and practiced their profession with dignity.

During the annual leave, Karunanidhi Annan and I would go to Thovoor, as it was also the season for reaping corn. As soon as the corn was cut I would go rat-hunting with Yesiah, Maduraiveeran, Thangarasu, Balraj and Minardas with our spade, sticks, etc. Annan would also come along with us. We would identify the rat holes and then dig them up. The clever rats would have two or three entries and exits. We would wait with our sticks at these these points and smoke them out. Sometimes they would lie within the holes in a semi-comatose stage. We would come back with lots of rats, big and small. On one such rat-hunting expedition, I hurt my big toe with the spade. To this day that toe does not have a proper nail. Whenever I look at it I think of the rat-hunting we did in Thovoor.

During Christmas, we would stage plays in the church at Thovoor. The church was built for the people of the cheri. Minardas, Balraj and Arpudam anna would take charge of the church festival. Once they had arranged for loudspeakers to play the songs. A particular song was played again and again. The Thovoor chairman, Madavan, wanted the person responsible for the prank to be brought to him. Minardas owned up to the prank and went to see him. Apart from the Pallans, Parayars and the Chakiliyars, there were only the Konars and Udayars in Thovoor. In fact the Konars were more in number. The cinema song – 'O joyous Konar, who went bankrupt of his intelligence' – was the reason for the problem.

'If it is a festival for the birth of Christ why don't you have devotional songs on Jesus? Are you trying to irritate us with the songs that ridicule the Konars? If you do so once again, things are going to become pretty bad for you,' warned the chairman.

The young men in the cheri on the other hand felt the Konars who constantly displayed their caste arrogance deserved it. The day would break every morning in the cheri with their arrogant voices calling the lower castes to work in their fields. The lower castes on the other hand were happy to accept these Konars as their masters and would proudly refer to 'my master's house' and 'your master's house' in their conversations. This is a type of slavery.

In my mother's birthplace, Keeranoor, Maravars would act like Brahmins. In my periamma's village, the Konars were the Brahmins. The Konars were not treated well by the Brahmins, and they in turn appropriated the caste arrogance of the Brahmins and showed it to the people of the cheri. During the rainy season, we would go rabbit-hunting across the slushy fields. The dogs would accompany us, and as we made inroads throught the thorny bushes the dogs would chase the escaping rabbits.

People used to sing the story of Michael Amma, as they worked on their lands. Her murder was something that deeply affected the people of the locality. I have heard my Annapushpam athachi say that Michael Amma's relatives still live in Thovoor, as she sang this song:

> Within the village were the high caste Udayars,
> Whose family was blessed with a pretty girl – the only king,
> Jesus' name was given to her.
> In the sandai of Salaigramam,
> In the shop of Sarkarai Nadar – Ah Michael Amma,
> We made promises.
> ……………………..
> ……………………..
> In your good caste,
> If I were to be born,
> Won't people curse me and talk about me!
> Tell me!
> O people of the God!
> Won't they ridicule me?

I'll tell you the story of Michael Amma. She was from the Pallar community. The boy was a Udayar. They fell in love when they were at school. But Michael Amma's family got her engaged to a person of their own community. One day, the Udayar boy followed her to the canal where she had gone to have her bath and confronted her saying, 'After having promised me that we will be husband and wife, are you trying to cheat me by marrying another?' She is said to have asked him, 'Will your people allow me to live if I get married to you?'

He tried to convince her that they could run away from their village and settle down in Devakottai.

'Even if we elope, your people will destroy my parents and my entire clan. Forget me and marry a girl in your own caste and live in peace', said Michael Amma. The next moment she was hacked to death with a sickle. Her head rolled to the ground. The boy surrendered to the police with his weapon in hand. He was imprisoned for fourteen years. Now he is a peon in the Kilanchunnai Hospital.

Ever since that murder, there has been no intercaste marriage in that area.

It was probably the after-effect of Michaelamma's murder, but there was a lot of hesitation to marry for love even within one's own caste. Thangarasu and Tamilarasi from the Thovoor cheri old street, studied together at the Salaiyur village school. By the time they finished their school final, they had developed a deep love for each other. No one knew about their love. Thangarasu was fair. So people called him Vellai Thangarasu. The results of the exams were out in the papers. Tamilarasi Akka had passed. Unable to afford an higher education she discontinued her studies. This was a common occurrence in most Dalit families.

Thangarasu ran away from the village one night, and did not return for nearly fifteen years. Tamilarasi Akka worked as a teacher in the local school. We heard that Thangarasu was in Bombay. Tamilarasi Akka got many offers of marriage from the surrounding villages. She refused the offers. Instead she took an active interest in getting her younger sister Kamalam married. The wedding took place in the Kilanchunai church. We had to travel in a bullock cart from Thovoor. I too went on this journey.

No one was privy to the fact that Thangarasu and Tamilarasi Akka were in love for over fifteen years. One day Tamilarasi Akka came to our house in Elayankudi and spoke to my annan Karunanidhi. Only then did I know about the relationship between her and Thangarasu. Thangarasu was taken to London by the shop owner for whom he worked in Bombay.

Tamilarasi akka didn't marry for many years. One day she brought a letter to our house and told us 'Thangarasu is coming to Thovoor. After he comes, we are getting married in a fortnight. As soon as we get married he is going to arrange for a passport for me and take me with him to London.'

The news caused quite a stir in Thovoor and the entire village was eager to see Thangarasu. Thangarasu came to our house in

Elayankudi dressed in a suit. I just couldn't recognise him. Tamilarasi Akka had come to our house the previous day itself.

Tamilarasi Akka's father was a good singer. Ever since he had had an attack of arthritis he just sat around with a bible in hand all the time. He was not alive when Thangarasu came back to the village. There was a bullock cart ready to take the guests from Elayankudi to Thovoor. Thangarasu went by the cart and Tamilarasi Akka took the bus. They got married. A few months later they left for London.

The love between Thangarasu and Tamilarasi Akka is the ideal one. I thought, 'It must be pretty difficult for intercaste marriages to happen if people of the same caste face so many difficulties to marry for love.' The idea that the village exists because of caste must change, only then will intercaste marriages be possible. If a Dalit and a girl of a different caste were to fall in love, they would not be able to live peacefully unless they get out of their village and went away to a town. Even then, in some places, they are not able to save their lives. The village high caste people, wanting to safeguard caste, would round up the couple who lived in the town and finish them off quietly.

Our cinemas do not talk about anything other than love. But love finds it difficult to survive in the everyday world. Actors and actresses become MLAs, MPs and chief ministers in our country. But the love they depict in the movies simply vanish into thin air in reality. People protest against movies these days. Some movements also do so. There is hope that changes would definitely happen.

4

As there are cheris in every village, so also in every cheri there would be a church. The houses in the cheris are mostly thatched huts, but the church alone would have a pucca building. The people whose roofs leak when it rains, would take refuge in the church.

My mother's place, north Keeranoor, had no shops and if one had to buy oil, soap, etc., they had to go to south Keeranoor, which was a mile away. There were a lot of Udayar houses here and the place had a beautiful church with tall spires. When people went to south Keeranoor to buy something they never carried any money with them. They would take things like paddy, chilies, tamarind and pulses, and exchange them for whatever they required.

Because every cheri had a church, very often the names of those living there were John, Joseph, Jeyaraj, Edward, Daniel, Bagyavathi and the like. The church bell would ring on Sundays alone. Even when I was a 'touser-clad' boy, I used to go to north Keeranoor whenever we had our holidays.

I had learnt to sing a lot of Christian songs at Keeranoor.

The village was surrounded by lush fields. To the north were the casuarina groves. Whenever I went to call my ammayi who would be working in the fields, the casuarina trees would sway in the wind like ghosts, making scary noises. On the east of Keeranoor lies Salaigramam. The irrigation tank would be brimming with water and we had to use a boat to cross it. I was very fond of this boat-crossing. Elayankudi is about seven miles to the west of Keeranoor. Keeranoor itself was situated beyond Valayanendal –

a Thevar stronghold. One can cross this village only after declaring one's caste to those men. Then we could have to deal with their dogs. From Valayanoor, there is a very good road leading to Keeranoor. But the road is meant to be used only by the higher caste. There is another path full of dirt and thorns, that's the one that leads to the Keeranoor cheri. I've never gone to my birthplace through the good road.

The village has a school. We used to go to this school to collect the milk powder and wheat that came from America. Most of the cheri children of this village would attend this school upto the third standard. Later, they were sent to the Christian hostels in Paramakudi, Madurai, Ramanathapuram, and Tarangambadi for further studies.

The cheri people observed Christmas and Deepavali with equal importance. Joseph and Daniel would go to Emaneshwaram and Paramakudi, and bring back pigs tied to their cycle carriers — not a bit worried about the squealing pigs. On the festival days, under the big tamarind tree near the church, they would spread out a mat and kill the pig by giving it a blow on its neck with the grain-pounding tool. The meat would be chopped up and portioned out. Some would pay money for it. Others would exchange it for chilies, paddy, tamarind, etc. On the days when the pigs are killed, every house would have pork and rice. Everybody ate pork meat in the cheri.

In the days when the irrigation tank has water in it, my ammayi would take me along with her and look for snails and slugs. She would bake them in a mud pot. We would use a kind of thorn to prise open the shells and eat the meat inside. During this season there would be snail shells heaped out in front of most houses. After having feasted on them we would use the shells as whistles. Dinner used to be only after 8 o'clock. Till then we would eat only slugs and snails. We usually had just a bit of cooked maize for dinner. We used only mud pots to cook our food. Somewhere someone might have a bronze vessel. The kozhambu would have settled down somewhere deep into the mud bowl. We have never really looked at the food we ate for dinner. With what little light we got from the kerosene lamp we ate our dinner. We would cook the greens that grew in the wild. Often we would pick the pumpkin leaves, clean and cook them; this would be served with our morning kanji. As we have our morning kanji, we would be worried about lunch – we may or may not have one. We may get cooked wheat in school once in a while. Often they wouldn't bother cooking it. They would give us some uncooked wheat and milk powder. We – boys of all castes – could be friendly with each other and play together only outside the village. Inside the village we had to address the upper caste person as, 'Ayya' and 'Sami'. The women were referred to as 'Nachiyar' or 'Aachi'. One had to call even those who were younger in age only thus. No one can call the upper caste boys or girls by their names: we could not touch them. We always had to stand at a distance.

As I grew older and became aware of many things, I did not like the idea of going to Keeranoor. Mustafa, Farook, Dulkarunai, Mohammed, Syed and Abu Bakar were all my friends in Salaiyur and Elayankudi. They were older than me and better built. However, I always addressed them in familiar terms. It was acceptable because I was a teacher's son. I could move around freely in Salaiyur and Elayankudi. I have never been prevented from going into the inner courtyard of a mosque. I have gone into the houses of Sheik Dawood, Abdul Kadar, Jehangir, and Khaja Mohiudeen and have eaten with them. This was not so in Keeranoor. If at all I wished to go there it was because of the love and concern shown by my ammayi and my mother's other relatives. Of course I stopped going there due to the problem between my mother and her brother Jovan, and a bad, unforgettable experience that I had there.

My ammayi gave me a bottle one day and asked me to buy oil from the shop at south Keeranoor. I took a boxful of paddy to give in exchange for the oil. It would have been more than three or four measures of paddy. I had the paddy on the head and the bottle in my hand.

The bottle had no stopper. To prevent the oil from spilling, the mouth of the bottle was closed with a small wood-chip. The bottle was held by a string that was wound around its neck. I gave the paddy in the shop and exchanged it for oil, and started walking towards north Keeranoor. It was then that this incident happened. There were fields on either side of the narrow bund. I had an empty box on my head and the oil bottle in one hand. There was someone walking on the same bund from the opposite side. I didn't pay any attention. I was humming a song to make my solitary travel easy. When the person who came in the opposite direction came near me I took one leg off the bund and kept it on the field and gave him space to walk past me.

Like lightning, it happened. A slap on the cheek caught me unawares and I screamed out for my mother. My ears rang and my cheek got swollen.

'Look at the cheek of the Paraya boy!' the man spat out, and then went on his way. It took me five minutes to come out of my state of shock. I put the box down and sat on the bund crying.

Since I had the string around the bottle's neck tightly woven around my hand, the oil did not spill. The bottle too was safe. After sometime I started walking back home. I had too many questions within myself. 'Why did that man beat me? What mistake did I do? Why did he call me a Paraya?' I didn't get any answer. I kept thinking about the incident as I walked. My cheek had swollen red by the time I reached north Keeranoor. I started crying the moment I saw my ammayi. As I told her what happened in between wracking sobs, it took her sometime to understand the whole story.

The moment she heard the entire story she said, 'See we belong to a Paraya household, and they are Maravars. When men and women of the high caste come, we need to stand at least eight feet away from them. We ought to step aside to give them way. That is why the man has beaten you.'

That day I decided I wouldn't go to any village where people spoke about caste while walking, speaking and standing. Not only to Keeranoor village but also to any village outside Elayankudi.

In 1964 there was a cyclone. Entire fields in Salaiyur went under water. We saw fish cheerfully leaping about on the roads. Khaja and I, along with the others, fished in the waters and had a good time. The radio kept repeating the news that Danushkodi was destroyed. We went to Pavadi. We were fascinated by the strange things brought in by the flood waters and now floating on the village pond. For a week folks never stirred out. My machan Muniyandi had just then come from Madurai to Elayankudi. Both of us went to see the good water pond overflowing at Sambi. In the Pudhur cannals water rushed out. We caught rabbits; we also saw, dead hens and goats floating in the water; a big log of wood too came floating down the water. We carried this back to our house with great effort. The rope cot that was made with this wood is still in our house. Jesudas Chithappa was lying on this cot for a long time, after his intestinal operation.

Sebastian and Kalairaj Anna were friends of my Muniyandi Machan. Sebastian Anna belonged to the Udayar caste. He joined the army and died in the Indo-China war. They sent home the clothes that he was wearing. My family mourned his passing for more than a week. Only when I grew older did I come to know that Sebastian Anna was an Udayar. Our house was in the Muslim street of Elayankudi. The casteless relationships that we had there makes me think of Islam as a great religion. The Muslims used to call the caste conscious others as 'Tamils'. Later when I used to speak at forums like 'The Tamils', 'The Tamil Movement', and 'The Tamil Conference', I recalled the Muslims' interpretation of the word 'Tamils'.

My mother was one of those who went from Keeranoor to the Ramanathapuram Schwartz High School hostel. It seems she used to walk with a trunk on her head for over ten miles to take the train. My mother had told me that she used to walk this distance along with her friends talking about all kinds of things. My mother had six children. Since she had studied till the eighth standard in those days she was offered many government jobs. Our father prevented her from taking up a job as she had to take care of the children. After we grew up a little and became more conscious of our poverty, we often asked her, 'Why Ma? Why didn't you take up the government jobs? If only you had gone to work we could have also lived like Kanagamani Cinamma and Devasigamani Chithappa's family.'

'It's all because of our father', Mother said.

If we made mistakes, Mother scolded us in English only. There is so much to say about our mother. I will come to it later.

I often wondered if it was because we became Christians that we had the opportunity to escape the caste-ridden village like Keeranoor by educating ourselves.

I still don't know how my father took on a second wife. My mother's sister is my father's second wife. My cinamma's name is Thavamani. She lived in Marandai, so my mother never allowed us to go there. Till we grew up we never knew how this Marandai village looked. We have never seen our mother and Cinamma speak. Father would go to Marandai every week. He used to go on Thursday evenings and come back on Saturday mornings. Fridays used to be the weekly holiday at Hamidiya School. Father used to ask us if we would go with him to Marandai, and Mother would stoutly deny permission saying, 'She would use black magic. So don't go there.' Marandai is about six miles from Salaiyur. My father has told us stories about his stint in the army, his participation in sports and drama, his smart military uniforms and the parades he had taken part in. It was a time when Dalits were recruited in the Indian military in large numbers. The well-to-do upper caste people never went to the military, since they had other options.

Father used to cover the six mile distance in an hour. He had the stride of a military man and the path would reverberate with the sound of his marching steps. I had to run to keep pace with his walk. My mother would announce my father's arrival just by recognising the sounds of his distinctive walk.

Thavamani Cinamma would come to the Saturday sandai at Elayankudi every now and then. She would bring palm fruits, kuzhipanniyaram and panangkizhangu for us. Anna and I would eat them without Mother's knowledge. Even when Mother asks us, 'Did you see her? Did she give you anything?' we would never disclose the fact. My anna and I would fight very often and he would beat me up. I would then tell on him to Mother. I would tell her that he ate the kuzhipanniyaram given by Marandai Cinamma. In turn, Anna would report on me too. Mother would beat us both and warn us saying, 'She will use black magic. Don't eat what she gives you. You will die.'

5

Everytime I think about my first visit to Marandai, I am pained by the thought. Before I tell you about my visit there, I should tell you about the place.

Father's thambi's name is Devasigamani. In the village they called him Chinna Azhagan. Even when the people of the cheri were given grand names, the people of the village always called them by a different name

Thatha's name was Karunanidhi. The villagers called him Karupa. Father's name is Azhagan alias Vedamanikam. The villagers called him Periya Azhaga. The higher caste people practiced discrimination even in names. Always the given name would be different from their moniker. Only the higher caste were privileged to be called by their sophisticated names.

Well, we've seen the politics behind names, now let's proceed to the village to know more about it. Thatha educated our father and his brothers. Thatha too was keenly interested in studies and made good use of what little opportunity he got. If a government official required signatures, of any two villagers on a petition, one of them would definitely be my thatha's. This was because Thatha was considered to be a learned man.

Muniyandi Machan often used to say, 'You should have seen Thatha donning a role in the koothu and delivering his dialogues. He was very impressive'

I remember Thatha singing certain songs to us. One of them was:

> Even if shielded from others,
> Or locked up in a golden pot,

> If the owner of the Heavens were to come,
> (Even if I am reluctant to go with him)
> Can He be denied?

Thatha was adept at writing songs, dialogues, and drafting letters and petitions to the government. In all these ways he was very useful to the upper caste. As he was better at the written word than the higher caste people, he was much respected in the village. In those days the postman used to deliver the medicine parcels which used to be sent to him from Salem and Coimbatore. I have heard the postmaster telling my Thatha, 'Karupa! I have to come all the way from Sooranam just for your sake.' Thatha was known in and around Marandai by the name Karupan. He treated the sick cattle in almost all the villages in that area. The medicines that were needed for treating the cattle used to come by parcels.

Thatha had a good physique. He always had on his person a medicine bag and a foot-long sickle. He wore ear-studs and his long hair would be gathered in a knot. He didn't go out to graze the cattle or play the drums or work as an agricultural labourer like others of our caste. As he tended to the sick cattle he was well known and respected by one and all.

Thatha would be asked to don a female role whenever the village puts up a play. Machan has told me often with deep regret that though Thatha had a voice and stature that would have suited any role, the upper caste people assigned only a woman's role to him. The upper caste people could not neglect him as a mere Paraya mainly because he was endowed with much intelligence. I have heard my Muniyandi machan tell me that Thatha had mistresses in many places. As Thatha got ready for the evening show, donning his grease paint, a hand would extend through the thatched wall. Thatha would accept the offerings of flowers, bangles, fruits, etc, made by those hands. The voice from the other side would whisper its identity saying it was so and so from Kalangaranga Kotai, or so and so from Sooranam, etc.

I liked only two people in Marandai village. One was my Thatha; another was Kandhan who studied with Muniyandi

Machan in his school and stayed with him in the Harijan Hostel. Kandhan belonged to the Pallar caste. Marandai cheri had five Chakiliyar, five Pallar and eight Parayar houses. Apart from them all the others in the village were Konars.

In the entire locality, my Thatha was the only one who had sent one of his children to Malaysia. The other two were trained to be teachers at Pasumalai. He made a living by treating cattle, and he used this money to give his sons an education. In addition to this, one more important information is, grandfather had an interest in Christianity. Many upper caste Maravar families in Sethur had converted to Christianity. Influenced by them the people in the cheri also became Christians. Therefore my father had two names – Azhagan and Vedamanikam. These people belonged to the C.S.I church. My father and his brothers got an education not merely because of Christianity but also because of the respect that was accorded to Thatha.

Father used to often mention some Thevar names like Pappathurai and Mappilaithurai. These were the Christian Maravars. The moment Marudupandian was hanged by the British, many Thevars converted to Christianity in order to work under the whites and to take up the management of Sivaganga province. They used to call the region Sethur–Marandai. There is a big Hindu temple in Sethur. When the Maravars in Sethur took to Christianity, the Parayas too became devout Christians. The Sethur Thevars helped Thatha when his sons were studying in Pasumalai. Otherwise it would not have been easy for them to get an education? In many cheris, because of conversion, people have been able to get an education. However to benefit from reservation they have registered themselves as Hindu Parayars. However, those people in the cheri who could not or did not want to study, they did not belong to Hinduism or Christianity. They worshipped their own family deities, and followed their traditional rituals. Our family deity, Muniayya temple is situated on the road to Marandai to Yerivayal, right adjacent to the canal. Occasionally we would worship him by scarifying cocks and goats and offering pongal. I have been here twice to take part in this ritual.

Our Thatha went to a thinnai school. But he would not be permitted to sit with the other boys because of his caste. He had to stand at a distance and listen to his teacher. He would often ask me to sing. He frequently spoke out his hope for the family saying, 'One of us should become a doctor.' Before grandfather died, Muniyandi Machan had become a doctor. Now and then he would come from Madurai to treat grandfather in Marandai. 'Ei, allow Gunasekaran to speak. He speaks well', he used to praise me to Muniyandi Machan. ' "I went to enjoy the breeze, but I have come back with a song" Ei, Gunasekara, there are nice songs these days in the cinema. See how this fellow who went to get breeze has come back with a song'. I still remember the way he used to enjoy this song.

I've gone to bathe only once in the Marandai canal. The water flowed like milk. The canal was dotted with tamarind trees on either side. I took off my shirt to have a dip as soon as I saw the water. Someone who was having his bath in that particular place asked me, 'Dei! Where are you from? Whose guest are you?'

'I am from here only. I am Karupan's grandson', I said. He said immediately, 'Oh! You are the boy from Elayankudi, is it? This place is meant for us. There, can you see that stone there? That is your area. Go to that place for your bath', he said.

The little square pond at Elayankudi-Salaiyur belongs to the Salaiyur Muslim Jamaat. A wall separated the bathing areas of the men and women. But there were no caste divisions marking the pond.

In my birth place, Marandai, since Thatha worked as a doctor tending to cattle, he was able to buy fields and groves, and he had planted palmyra, tamarind and mango trees. Even now we have property in our village, that grandfather had bought, and what he had inherited from his father.

If we went around Chandra canal, Palaiaramba field, Parayan Kollai, Keezhvayal and the mango groves we would have made a trip around the entire village.

To the south of our house, there was a common water pond with fresh water. One day I was lying under the tamarind tree on the banks of the pond on a hot afternoon and had dozed off. I woke up suddenly when I heard the sounds of wood being chopped. An eight-year-old boy was hacking the branches of a tree that was full of flowers and tender fruits to feed his goats. Incensed, I asked him, 'Dei! Why are you cutting away the flowers and the tender fruits of our tree?' That was all. In a fraction of a second he slapped me across my face. Even before I could react he ran away rather fast.

As I was thinking, 'Did I say anything wrong? Why did he slap me? And why is he running away so fast?', I saw him come back with four or five big men.

Even as I was looking at them approaching me, Thatha came running to my side. He pleaded with them saying, 'Ayya! ayya! The boy has come from the town and he does not know our village ways. Please forgive him ayya'. He fell at their feet, full length, begging them to forgive me.

'Dei Elayankudi boy, it is because of Karupan that you've escaped today, otherwise we would have skinned you alive and rubbed salt on you. Do you know whom you have addressed as "Dei"? We will cut your tongue. Are you aware of the difference between your caste and ours? You've lost your mind having made friends with the Elayankudi Muslim fellows. Be careful and know your caste before you speak. Otherwise we would make you scarce. You have the audacity to address one of us as 'Dei', is it? Karupa, teach him propriety. If he speaks like this again, we wouldn't bother about who he is.' They intimidated me thus and left the place. Life came back to me only after they had gone away a little distance. Then Thatha caressed my cheek and said, 'See boy! Even if they are younger to us we have to show them respect. The fellows in this village are brainless. Caste arrogance has been increasing as days go by. I don't know when these fellows will realise their folly.' Thus the two times that I was slapped across the face, both in my father's village and mother's village, were due to caste issues.

I was then doing my B.A. The Trichy All India Radio would often broadcast the folk songs I had sung. Since the relay used to be after 6:30 in the evening, the people who came back to the village after working in the fields the whole day, would listen to it on the Panchayat radio.

> By the side of the road stood the lady of my heart,
> Clad in a saree with roses on it.
> Shall I wait? –
> Or shall I go?
> Oh cruel kinswoman
> If I touch you, would I affect you? – Hey lady!
> If I touch you, would I affect you?

Before and after the broadcast of my song they would announce the song was sung by Elayankudi K.A. Gunasekaran. I had the opportunity to sing on the radio while still at the Sivaganga College because of poet Meera. In both my village and college, I had a very good name because of this.

Once when my father had brought me to Marandai, something strange happened. In the dead of the night there was a big noise, accompanied by somebody's hard breathing. Scared, I got up to see what was the cause. My cinamma Thavamani was running here and there with a broom in hand. People from some houses brought out their lamps and were watching the fun. 'Dei! A wicked devil has gotten into the village. Chase him away,' she shouted and went into a Konar house, and woke up a fellow sleeping in his house. 'Come out! Why did you come to take away my son? Go away devil, go', she screamed and started beating him up in the courtyard of his house with a broom. Afterwards she ran back to her house and fell down in a fit of faint. The people around sprinkled water and smeared her forehead with holy ash. She slept off tired. The people in the cheri decided that Thavamani was possessed by god. Next morning my chithappa

Devasigamani ridiculed her saying. 'Look at the person on whom God descends. In the name of god, she goes into the Konar's house and beats him up with a broom. If it wasn't for god, can she have entered the Konar house?' All of us – Munniyan Mama, Veeran Chithappa and Kandhan Annan – laughed and ridiculed her for a long time.

One day, early in the morning, I was still lying on the cot in our courtyard. Even as I was deciding about whether to get up or not, I heard a voice chiding me, 'Hey! Who is this sleeping even after the sun has come out?' No one in Marandai had ever addressed me in such disrespectful terms. When I got up I found an upper caste man standing with a spade in hand asking people to come and work in his fields. I continued to be seated on the cot.

He looked at me and said, 'While I am standing who do you think you are to sit in such a leisurely manner on the cot? Get up!' I got up slowly. The moment he recognised me, he said, 'Oh! You are the fellow who sings on the radio, is it?'

I nodded my head in assent.

'You were born in Marandai. Your father, your grandfather are from this place, but you call yourself on the radio as Elayankudi Gunasekaran. You after all only went to Elayankudi for livelihood. Henceforth call yourself Marandai Gunasekaran on the radio. Our village too should become famous', he said.

'Just because I was born here you ask me to identify myself with Marandai. I was born here, but grew up in Elayankudi. The Elayankudi Muslims are very loving towards me. They ask us to eat with them when they have celebrations in their houses. I address them as Kaka, Mamu and Mami, like they were my own relatives. Caste was never a barrier. And never did they, even after knowing our caste, discriminate us. Whereas in my birthplace, Marandai, apart from the tree, the soil and the house that we own, the relationship between living beings is fractured by caste. Caste has divided people into the village and the cheri. In Elayankudi, all people are my relatives. Whereas here, only the tree and the soil are close to me. How can I mention Marandai on the radio when I share no ties with the people here? That is why I call myself on the radio as Elayankudi Gunasekaran. For me that seems to be the right thing to do. I played, studied and had friends only in Elayankudi. It is difficult for me to think of Marandai as my place since I have never been given access to the upper caste streets in the village,' I said, explaining to him my stance. He on the other hand tried to escape criticism by saying, 'Unless, many things change, Marandai would not be as you want it to be.'

A cart heading to the cheri couldn't reach the place even though there was a cart track. I don't know where else such unfairness would exist. This happened in my birthplace, Marandai. I was in the fifth or sixth standard; I am not sure when this happened. One could only walk to reach Salaiyur from Marandai, a distance not less than eight miles. It was our Chithappa's wedding. The bride and the bridegroom were brought back to Marandai in a cart. Because I was a small boy, I was given a place to sit in the cart.

Our cinamma's name is Kanagamani. Like my chithappa, Devasigamani, she was also trained to be a teacher. She was stylish and good-looking. I kept looking intently at her saree, blouse, bangles, ear rings and the new thali around her neck. Observing me looking at her, my cinamma sat me on her lap and showed me her trinkets. The cart went through Pudhur, Sothukudi and Sathani to reach Sethur. My father, Thatha, Muniyandi Machan, his annan Arasan, and thambis Malaikannu, Thiagarajan (Jayaraj) and Marandai Munniyan Mama, were all walking behind the cart. Kanagamani Cinamma's mother was in the cart with us. This lady and Kakan Thatha's wife were sisters. Thumbaipatti, near Meloor, is their village.

Cinamma's father, Kannamirtham, had worked under the English as a cook. It seems they shifted to Madurai to educate the children. Kakan Thatha was then the minister in charge of the law and order in the Congress cabinet. The minister's sister-in-law's daughter was Kanagamani cinamma. In short, a girl from the minister's family was being brought back to the village.

The cart track leading to Marandai village from Sethur goes straight into the village. There was a general cheerfulness about having neared the village. But having set foot in the village their happy conversations stopped and and there was a kind of a caution on their faces. Later they told each other the events unfolded exactly as they had expected. For in a distance, ten to fifteen men from the Konar community barricaded the road, preventing the cart from entering the village.

Our thatha walked briskly upto them and asked, 'What is this ayya! This is an alliance with the minister's daughter. We have fixed a cart to bring the bride and bridegroom in a dignified manner to our village. Both of them are trained to be teachers. Can't they both go by cart?'

'Sure the cart can go, Karupa. Who said no? But let the cart go to your cheri by a different path. Don't you know that this road goes to the upper caste street?' asked a person who stood barricading the road.

Thatha reasoned, 'But ayya, haven't we driven the cart on your road with your people sitting in it?'

'Look here Karupa; don't be impertinent! We can go into our streets, but you want us to mutely witness your people ride the cart and make a grand entrance into our street? Don't keep talking unnecessarily. Take a different route, and reach your homes safely.'

Father went forward to plead the cause, saying, 'Ayya! Is this the kind of treatment you give to us – people who have been serving your families for generations.'

'Azhaga, will caste go away if you are learned? You want us to forget the village custom because you are a little educated?"

The bridegroom, Devasigamani chithappa, tried to get off the cart to talk to the Konars. He was prevented by the others. 'We will take care of this. You are a newly wed. Keep calm', they said, trying to pacify him.

Thatha asked, 'Ok! What is your final decision?'

'We have already stated it, and there is nothing to change.'

'Why ayya, does this cart track end when it enters your settlement? Does it not extend upto Sokhapadapu? Isn't this the road for Sokhapadapu people to reach Sethur or the lake and the fields? The government has ear-marked it as the common passage for all. How can you then think of it as yours', said Thatha.

Two of them tried to beat up Thatha, saying all kinds of things to him. Father tried to block them, and two or three of the Konars themselves prevented their men by saying, 'Don't hurt Karupan'.

Our relatives who were waiting for an opportunity for a fight ran to get sticks from the tamarind tree and the neem tree. Our grandfather pushed them away by saying, 'Hey! Throw the sticks away you fools! They know only that much. Leave it. Turn the cart away. Hmmm….get going.' These relatives gave a lot of respect to my Thatha and his sons. Hence the moment he ordered them they threw down the sticks and came to the cart.

'There is a cart track running through the village, but there is none that leads to the cheri. This is the first time that a cart is coming into the cheri and this is our first experience. So, let us lay our track for the cart to go to our cheri. Go and get your spades and crow-bars. We have to lay the track through the fields, and we will have to level out the bunds', said grandfather, and even before he could finish, people ran to the cheri to get what he wanted.

Some person from Madurai said, 'Shall we ask the bride and bridegroom to walk to the cheri?'

But Muniyan Mama said, 'No, let them not get down from the cart. Whatever happens the cart should go to our cheri.' Loudspeakers were blaring out songs from the house that was celebrating the wedding in the cheri. The song that was playing when this incident took place was:

> Is the tree a burden to the land?
> Is the branch a burden to the tree?
> Is the fruit a burden to the creeper?
> Can one's own child become a burden to a mother?

The men and women who were waiting to welcome the bride and bridegroom rushed out joyously when they heard of their arrival. Having heard about the incident, they wondered aloud 'When will these upper caste people change their attitude?' They joined in the work of laying the road for the cart, all the while scolding the Konars and admiring the newly weds. In a little while, for the first time, a cart entered the Marandai cheri.

The Konars had built a few houses in the cheri at Marandai. Even then our Thatha was looked up to for having built a house with tiled roof. The newly weds went into the tiled house. Thus my entry into my native place was tinged with caste.

Outside our house we had a thatched hut and a few tamarind trees. The well, which supplied potable water was behind our house, and so was the cheri people's graveyard. Beyond that were our dry lands, full of thickly grown thorn trees.

All these things in Marandai appealed to me for it was so different from Elayankudi or Salaiyur. More than all these things my Thavamani cinamma's love drew me to the place.

She would to say, 'When you were still a baby, your mother just left you in the crib and went away in a huff. I am the one who fed you.' Thus her affection for me made me want to come to Marandai often.

I had come to Marandai once when I was in the tenth standard, and twice or thrice when I was in college. My athai's daughter Sebastiamma has come to our Elayankudi-Salaiyur house once or twice when I was still in high school there. She was then studying in seventh or eighth standard in Devadiyar Pattinam. Muslim women in our village never spoke with unknown men. They would cover their heads, and talk from a distance even to their relatives. Young girls would hide themselves. Since I came from such a background I would avoid talking to my cousin Sebastiamma. She used to make efforts to talk to me, but I would run away feeling quite self-conscious. She would stay with us at Elayankudi for one or two days and go to see our Thatha in Marandai. The cinema tent was quite close to our house. The songs and dialogues would be heard clearly. One day I was sleeping after watching a late-night show.

Next day Sebastiamma tried talking to me. I was pretty much disconcerted. She said, 'It seems you sing very well. Mama told me. Why don't you sing a song for me from the cinema that you saw last night?' I was tongue-tied. In a little while Sebastiamma herself started singing

> In the Murugan temple at Chendur – I heard a news
> At dawn as the cock-crowed – I heard a song

Sebastiamma must have heard the cinema songs sitting at home itself. She sang it for me. I ran away overcome by shyness. I used to feel shy even to look at her face. I knew that she never felt so by the way she approached me and talked to me. Her mother's name is Rakhi and their place is Aakavayal.

Soon after Sebastiamma's father passed away, her mother too died. In her death bed she asked my father, much as in a cinema, to assure her that he would marry her daughter off to one of his sons. One day my father told Muniyandi Machan, 'She is much younger than Karunanidhi so we should get her married off to Gunasekaran.' My cousin disagreed saying, 'Mama, make Gunasekaran study further. Let us look for a groom for Sebastiamma in some other place.' I think it was only after she listened to such talk that Sebastiamma tried to get close to me.

Sebastiamma was an orphan. Often she would come to see my Thatha in Marandai. Once while I had gone to Marandai, she stood on the banks of the fresh water pond and asked me to give a hand in lifting the pot to her head. She had later told Muniyandi Machan that I had run away without helping her. He asked me as to why I did so. Only then I confessed, 'In Elayankudi young girls don't talk to men.' He replied, 'That is something followed by Muslim women. In our community we can see each other and talk.'

After he said so I decided to talk to Sebastiamma, the next time I met her. The next time I met her she was with her husband

and two children in her sister Yesamma's house at Puliyadithammam.

My mind carried the smart figure of Sebastiamma in skirt and dhavani, as I saw her in Marandai. But when I saw her in Puliyadithammam, I was taken aback. The image I had in my mind was not there in front of me. I felt sorry for Sebastiamma who was emaciated after going to Andaman and having had two children.

I had felt quite bad about not having helped her with the water pot in Marandai. It is because of the influence of the Muslim ways on my thinking which had prevented me from liking Sebastiamma who liked me.

Thus my birthplace Marandai was a happy thing in my memory because of love, affection and care I received from my Thavamani cinamma, Satyabalan, Saradha, Karupan Thatha and Sebastiamma.

Muniyandi Machan has often related to me an incident that happened while he was at the medical college. The Konars of Marandai were very careful about maintaining caste distinctions. From Elayankudi to Sooranam there was only one bus. It used to reach Sooranam via Salaigramam. From Sooranam, Marandai was three miles by walk via Sokhapadapu. The cart track between Sokhapadapu and Marandai was a lengthier route. The short cut was through the fields, bunds and canals. In between there were two or three fallow lands. Only when it rained did these lands have water. Otherwise they used to be full of thorn trees. Muniyandi Machan, who was doing M.B.B.S in Madurai, had taken this route one day to see our thatha in Marandai. It was then that this incident happened.

It was very hot. There was a person ploughing the field. My machan used to sing very well. M.G.R had in fact given him a gift of Rs. 10000 after listening to his singing. This was flashed in all the papers. Like the sound of the bells preceeding the oncoming elephant, his songs would be heard in the village even as he was walking through the fields. People would enquire after his well-being as he made his way to the village.

One day this incident took place. Even as Muniyandi Machan was wondering as to why the man who was ploughing was not listening to his song or greeting him, the man fell down with an epileptic attack. His body was wracked by spasms and fits. Muniyandi Machan identified him as a Konar belonging to Marandai. He detached the plough from the ox and made him hold on to it. Because spasmodic fits would stop by touching iron, he made him do that. It was very hot; Machan lifted him up and laid him down under a tree, took a hand towel from his bag and fanned him with that. The man still did not regain his consciousness. He took a little bit of water from his porridge vessel and splashed it on his face.

The water brought back the man to his senses and as he opened his eyes Machan said, 'Ayya, it's me Muniyandi, Karupan's grandson. You fell down with fits and I brought you here and laid you under the tree till you got back your consciousness.' The moment he finished recounting what happened, the Konar who had regained not only his consciousness but also his arrogance said, 'Who asked you touch me? How can you, a Parayan, touch me?'

'Ayya, I was worried if anything would happen to you,' told my machan. Immediately the man retorted saying, 'What would have happened? What if I die? Stand away! It is your arrogance due to education. You mean to say I got this fits only today? It has been with me ever since my birth. Let us talk about this in the Panchayat this evening.'

Muniyandi Machan walked towards the house at a fast pace thinking to himself, 'What is this? Instead of making a deity, I have made a monkey.' Most of the people assembled in the Panchayat were of the opinion that it was sheer arrogance which made Muniyandi Machan touch the Konar's porridge vessel and carry him to the shade. Since thatha was a cattle doctor and much respected, the Panchayat had to dismiss the case, but not without asking Muniyandi Machan to prostrate before the Panchayat, seeking their forgiveness.

We have often recounted this incident and laughed. On the way from Thovoor to Marandai, Kalangaran Kotai (Kalankathaan Kottai) is situated. If we walk without stopping anywhere we would reach Marandai in two hours time. I have walked to Marandai with my cinamma twice or thrice, and have walked alone once or twice. One time when I was making this journey alone, dusk had settled and I was not able to make out the road. Generally during the planting season, we will have only a dirt path across the fields. During the harvest time we will walk in the direction of the villages through the fields. It was planting season the day I happened to walk alone. I started running on the dirt path across the fields. It looked as though I was bitten on the leg by something when I crossed the canal. There was a mild pain. I panicked and thought, 'Aha! Looks as if a snake has bitten me. If it is was a cobra or a bandit krait or any other poisonous snake, I would in a little while froth at my mouth and die.'

Dusk was fast approaching and I walked as fast as I can. 'Adede! No one would know in this darkness if I lie here frothing at the mouth. Only at dawn people might stumble upon me. If I die, my body would lie here eaten by the foxes.' I thought so as I was running. 'Let me die after I reach Marandai', I told myself and ran. I slowed down only on seeing Cinamma. Panting, I told her about my leg being bitten. Cinamma gave me a little jaggery and asked me, 'Is it sweet?'

I said, 'yes'.

'Okay. It is nothing. May be a scorpion bit you. Show me where you felt the bite.' I showed my leg and heaved a sigh of relief when she said after a thorough examination with the help of a wick lamp, that there was no bite mark.

If I had to go to the shops at night in Elayankudi, I would sing loudly to myself or repeat a cinema dialogue to overcome my fear as I ran back home. I used to be dead scared even when the streets were lit by bright lights. My heart still misses a beat when I think of the day I made the journey all by myself from Thovoor to Marandai cutting across fields without any light. If only it had been day time all those working in the fields would have asked me, 'Where are you from? Whose house are you going to?' I would have answered all this and more before I reached the village. Any new comer who entered the village will have to disclose his caste identity before entering the village.

Thus our country is still in a state where village and caste are inseparable. Gandhi made much of these villages only! If I tell you the ridiculous incident that my Machan told me, you would certainly agree with what I say. Muniyandi Machan would be called by all our relatives as Doctor. They called him Doctor Machan and Doctor Thambi. He was brought up by my Thatha in Marandai. Upto to high school he was educated by my father. My father and Chithappa struggled much to get him educated in a college.

While Machan was doing B.Sc. second year or third year in Sivagangai, he got a seat in M.B.B.S. It was said that Kakan Thatha had helped to get the seat. Even as he was in his house surgeon year, the Marandai Konars would take a bus to Madurai to consult him if they had even an ordinary ailment like stomach ache. Machan would also take good care of them as they came from his native place.

The Marandai Konars would call him Doctor Thambi when they saw the nurses, doctors, compounders and attenders greet him in Madurai big hospital, as he walked in wearing his white coat, with a stethoscope around his neck. After they became better they would leave for their homes. When Machan went with them to see them off at Madurai bus stand, they would say, 'Muniyandi! Shall we then take leave? You get the medicines from the doctor whom you referred us to when you next come to Marandai.' Machan would say, 'Ayya, if you have any other problem come straight to the hospital, I will take care.' They would then leave saying, 'Ok Muniyandi, we will go. Would you like us to take a message for Karupan? See you then Muniyandi....' Those who called him Doctor Thambi in Madurai big hospital, would call him 'Muniyandi' by the time they reach Madurai bus stand. If the same people saw him at the Elayankudi market place they would say, 'What Muniyandi or Ei Muniyandi! When did you come from Madurai? When are you likely to come to Marandai?' At Marandai village the respect would deteriorate further. Thus Machan has often told me the painful truth of how the respect that one receives in the city becomes much diminished in the village. I would jokingly tell him to prescribe the wrong medicines when the upper caste fellows of this village go to him for treatment, thereby complicating their illness. But he used to say, 'The medical profession is a life-saving profession and it insists that we should save even the life of our enemy. Those fellows will change. How long do you think they will be without changing? Otherwise people like us should get educated and change them.'

Machan and I used to love walking to Marandai. We would drink toddy as we walked through the fields, and used to sing songs like –

> Sangam will live – Tamizh and
> Madurai city will flourish,
> Abundance with grace will come,
> From elegant Meenakshi.
> There is no other god,
> Like mother.

At home I used to sit on Machan's chest and sing after him. He would say 'Open your throat and sing with ease. The voice must have the tenor of a bell. Don't sing through the nose.' While walking through the fields, he used to correct whatever I sang and also teach me. It is this practice that Machan gave me at home and on the fields and grounds that has made me known to the people as a singer.

My voice ripened because of the songs that I sang on those days when I walked from Marandai, Thovoor, Sooranam and Elayankudi. After the exams Machan would take me around saying, 'If we go to Papa Thangachi's house they would cook a chicken for us. If we went to Sebastiamma's place a chicken would be killed in our honour and if you went to Kalangaran Kotai there again they would kill a chicken for our meal.' Machan would take me with him tempting me with those chickens. We walked – toddy and songs keeping us company. Everywhere our relatives used to give him much respect because Machan had done M.B.B.S. In our family he was the first doctor. My Thatha had much affection for Machan. He was a cattle doctor, and Machan gave medical aid to human beings. The dream of my Thatha was realised through Machan when he became a doctor. Muniyandi Machan was born in Uridikottai. He was the son of father's only elder sister. My father and Devasigamani Chithappa used to send money for Muniyandi Machan, whether they had money for their own family expenditure or not. My mother and Kanagamani Cinamma would quarrel with them often saying, 'When we do not have enough money for our own expenses, why do you send money to your sister's son?' Father and Chithappa were keen on having a doctor in the family. Karunanidhi Annan was better at studies than me. After the Pre-university exams he stood firm on doing M.B.B.S.

'It is so difficult to find the money to educate Akka's son to become a doctor. You too want to study is it? You better study something else', told father. It was a big loss and grief when that Doctor Machan died at a very young age having been affected by diabetes. In the graveyard of Uridikottai there is a grave with a cross on top of it. All those belonging to that village agreed unanimously to have a Christian tomb amidst the Hindu graves for Doctor Machan. Muniyandi Machan married into a Christian family of Palayamkottai. His wife's name is Hema, and she used to have a Bible in her hand always.

Machan, who sang songs on Lord Muruga and Vinayaka changed completely and started talking only about the Bible and church. Till his death he did something in secret that his wife never approved of. Since he was very friendly with T.R. Mahalingam he used to don the king's role in the plays of Sankaradas Swamigal in the Madurai stage artist's club. He used to lie to his wife that he had a surgery to do in the night and would go to various villages to act. He would get back home in the morning. In the information bulletin of the dramas his name would be Manimaran instead of Muniyandi. He introduced me to T.R. Mahalingam when I went to Madurai, and asked me to learn music from him. T.R. Mahalingam Sir would always be chewing betel leaves. Even while signing he would have it at one corner of his mouth. I asked him once, 'You sing so well. Do you take anything special apart from betel leaves?' He replied, 'That is a secret. Why do you want all that? You have a naturally good voice. Whatever I take will spoil your good voice.' However I kept trying to find out what was it that he took to keep his voice so good. T.R. Mahalingam Sir not only did not tell me the secret, but died without revealing it to anybody.

It was in Madurai that M.G.R wrote out a cheque for Rs. 10000 for the song that Muniyandi Machan sang. And it was here that he made friends with T.R. Mahalingam. The Marandai upper caste people gave respect to him only in Madurai. But in Marandai he would be addressed in common terms. Yes, Machan had certainly realised the terrible dance of the caste devil in the villages. The caste devil was a bit more restrained in the city.

6

Meera, they say, loved the flute-playing Kannan. But our poet Meera loved me for my voice. To celebrate the tenth anniversary of the Madurai University, an inter-collegiate competition was conducted. A representative was sent from each college. I was sent from Dr. Zakir Hussain College of Elayankudi. I bagged the first prize in the music competition and the second prize in mono-acting.

Subsequently there was a competition held for Bharathiyar's songs for the colleges in Ramanathpuram district. The audition for that took place in Ramanathapuram. There was an audition in my college to select the participant for that competition. I was one of the twenty who registered for the competition. I was in the first year of B.A. in the Sivaganga Mannar Duraisingam College. We were blatantly segregated by our caste in this place.

Every year fights would break out between the Thevar students of Ramanathapuram and Usilampatti. However, it would be the students from the lower castes whose heads would get broken in these fights. College would close interminably due to these caste fights. At the time of exam, officers and professors would interfere and would have the college re-opened. In such a famous college, the audition took place in the classroom on the second floor. I had been practising for this competition for more than twenty days.

Do you know who gave me training? It was the actor-singer T.R. Mahalingam of Chozhavandan who sang in his inimitable tenor in numerous movies. In those days he was staying in a lodge in Madurai. He was acting in plays staged in villages in and around

Madurai – plays like Valli Thirumanam, Nandanar, Kovalan, Sathyavan Savithri and other plays of Sankaradas Swamigal. He had given me training. When I sang before him, he said, 'Nobody can beat you. You will become a big singer like me.' So I practised continuously in the barren, cactus-growing open lands at Sivaganga, hoping to sing better in the competition.

I got up when the call, 'K.A.Gunasekaran, B.A. Economics', was heard. The other caste boys who identified me, booed loudly. I didn't lose my cool. I went to the stage, greeted the audience and started singing. The booing continued. The professor, who was judging the competition asked me to continue. I started humming :

> Ah……ah……ah
> Aah…..aah…….aah…..

Those who were causing the disturbance also raised their voices:

> Ah……Ah…

When I started the song with a lot of emotions in my voice:

> On the banks of the waterfalls – on the southern corner,
> In the Champak garden,
> I waited for you in the moonlight,
> You said you would come with your maid.
> You have not kept you word – my darling,
> My chest heaves…

The people in the first and second rows started listening to me as I continued with the song. They shushed those who were behind them. As I sang,

> Wherever I look – I see a maiden
> just like you…,

there was silence in the classroom. I continued my song :

> My body burns – my darling,
> My body does burn – my head whirls,
> And gives me trouble – my darling,
> Aah…..aah…..aah….

I sang plaintively:

> Kannamma, Kannamma,
> Kannamma, Kannamma.

When I finished rendering this Bharathiyar song, the students clapped enthusiastically till I went back to my place and sat down. Many came to me and said, 'You would win'. I have often thought about that day when people pushed caste aside, and appreciated me for my talent.

The entire college read the announcement on the notice board that K.A. Gunasekaran was taking part in the district level music competition. That day when I turned the pages of my notebook to take down notes, I found in a beautiful handwriting a small note saying,

Dear Gunasekaran,

Forgive me. I kept shouting, not allowing you to sing. Only later did I notice the sweetness of your voice. I underestimated you, having only your caste in mind and not taking into account your true talent.

With affection,
Athiappan.

Samidoss showed the page to everyone. I had many upper caste boys as my fans. I showed what was written in the notebook to Professor Meera, who was the head of the department of Tamil at the Sivaganga College. 'All boys are good. It's because of a few that the college gets a bad name', he said.

A district level music competition was held in one of the colleges of Ramanathapuram. Meera was one of the judges. When my name was called I sang with the same intensity the song that I sang for the audition. I was much appreciated after my performance. I realised from the thunderous claps that the first prize was mine. Many girls who had come to sing at the competition from the various colleges in Ramanathapuram district too congratulated me. Some were angry with me for not allowing their college to win the prize. A bus load of boys and girls had come from Virudhunagar College to take part in the competition. Professor Meera took me along to introduce me to someone in the Ramanathapuram College who wished to meet me.

I entered the principal's room, where the judges of the competition were having tea. Professor Meera shook my hands. The principal and the others too shook my hands, and announced that I had won the first prize.

When I returned to Sivaganga the next day, the peon brought a message to my class saying that the principal wanted to see me. Meera was there with the principal. Not only did they congratulate me, but they had also nominated me as the cultural secretary of the N.S.S. Unit and the college.

From that day I regularly performed at all the college functions. Since I secured the first mark in the college in Tamil, Meera made me the secretary of the Bharathi Club the following year. Until this time, no student belonging to the oppressed class had held such posts in the history of the college. Despite knowing that I belonged to the Dalit community, Professor Meera took me to his house and offered me food. Publications like Annam and Agaram, which were spoken of much in Tamil Nadu in those days, were his. Therefore I had the opportunity of getting to know many writers and reviewers in Tamil Nadu. I used to proof-read many books. It was through him that I got to read many Tamil literary texts. It was Poet Meera who introduced me to many writers like late T. Krishna, Congress leader V. Subramanian, Professor Solomon Pappaiah, K.R., Poet Bala, Professor N. Dharmarajan, Poet Abdul Rahman, Thothatri, Tamizh Annal, the assembly speaker, K. Kalimuthu, and others.

There was a poetry reading contest at Manamadurai. Meera headed it. Comrade Gandarvan, M. Jameson and I read our poems. Meera enjoyed that poem which I read in that forum arranged by Tamil Nadu Art and Literature Club.

> Thinking that if I weep and talk it out,
> The burden would reduce – I,
> Come to weep and speak.

> But sorrow chases me
> And chokes me.....

I started in this manner and concluded the poem by saying:

> The learned are celebrated wherever they go,
> But today,
> The learned are received with contempt wherever they go.

The poem was the voice of an unemployed graduate. Meera appreciated my poem. Later I was invited to participate in a poetry forum in Ramanathapuram. Meera used to send me to Madurai to invite Solomon Pappaiah, Tamizh Annal and others to participate in the Sivaganga College function. I felt proud that I was sent on such errands in those days.

Meera taught me and guided me through the various stages of printing the invitations, arranging the meetings, speaking in a forum, etc. We used to discuss the happenings of the day after every meeting got over. We would entertain our guests at the Shanmuga Bhavan hotel situated near the Sivaganga palace and after putting them in their respective buses, we would just walk with our cycles upto Annam Publications office, talking about various things.

A teacher got married at Manamadurai. I asked Meera to lend me money to give him a gift. He gave me ten rupees for the bus fare and a translation by Professor Dharmarajan, entitled, *Will the moon come and sing* and asked me to give that as the gift. He added, 'People should get into the habit of buying and reading books. We should start a movement for it.'

The college used to remain closed interminably due to caste fights now and then. On those occasions I used to take money from Meera Sir to go to my place. Most of the boys, belonging to the Dalit community, will not have money. I used to make a list of those who required help to reach their homes, and distribute the money in the scrub jungle nearby. Only after ensuring that those who took the money have boarded the buses to go home, I used to board my bus to Elayankudi. My friend Samidoss, helped me in this task, and we both would be the last ones to leave.

Meera took the N.S.S students to do relief work in Nagapattanam after the town was ravaged by a storm. On the way back, he had given an interview at the Trichy Radio Station. After listening to his interview, I expressed my desire to sing on the radio. He gave me a letter and asked me to meet his friend Vijaya Thiruvengadam, who was then the director of the Trichy Radio Station. The next day I went to Trichy and showed him the letter. He took me immediately to the recording theatre. I looked at the recording theatre with wonder and awe. So far my world had revolved around huts, rented houses and college. I was happy to have come so far as to step into a radio station and the recording theatre. Thiruvengadam Sir asked me to sing and he recorded what I sang from a different room with a glass enclosure:

> The sun and moon will soon light up the world,
> In the dead of the night, in the sandalwood hill,
> I yearn to make you mine,
> Hey, my April thrush – Hey, my April peacock.

The last three lines were recast by Meera. A week later the folk songs that I had sung were relayed on the radio with my name attached to Elayankudi. Those who heard my song on the radio, in the village and the college, praised me and congratulated me. On Vijaya Thiruvengadam's recommendation, I was called often to sing on the radio. It was as Elayankudi Gunasekaran that I sang most of the folk songs. I was introduced to the public only by that name.

Later I released audio albums entitled *Thanane, Mannin Padalgal, Manuzhangada, Manuzhi* and *Dalit Muzhakam*. For all these later attempts the radio gave me my first encouragement. My first experience with the media was my Trichy performance.

Meera often used to talk about K.R's writings. Without Meera, the world would not have known K.R. *Vetti (Dhoti), Kathavu (Door), Kiraavuku Vantha Kadithangal (Letters for K.R.)* were some of K.R's writings that Meera published. I sought Meera's advice for my higher studies after B.A. He asked me to do postgraduation in Tamil in Madurai Thyagaraja College.

That was the college which had brought out students like brother Abdul Rahman, P. Jayaprakasam, K. Kalimuthu, Elambharati (Tulasi), and others. Many who studied here took part in the Hindi agitation, and many more are famous in Tamil Nadu today. I gave the recommendation letter from Meera Sir to the Principal S.B. Annamalai. Meera had written:

> Under your Tamil shelter
> He wishes to learn its literature
> Both the college and he
> Would mutually benefit by this association

I got a seat in M.A. Tamil. Saiva Siddhanta was one of the subjects offered. The Marxist ideologies of Professor Meera and Professor Dharmarajan had had its impact on me, and I did not wish to study Saiva Siddhanta. I asked Meera if I should transfer to Karaikudi Azhagappa College where Kamba Ramayanam was the optional paper. He told me, 'If we do not like something we should refuse it only after knowing all about it. We should not say no to it without knowing anything about it'. I prepared myself to do Saiva Siddhanta. I learnt karagam and kavadi from Om Periyaswami during the first year. I went with him to Delhi in 1981 to take part in the Republic Day celebration. Indira Gandhi was the prime minister then. All the artists were invited to dinner at her house.

Indira Gandhi shook hands with me and enquired in English, what I was doing? When I said I was studying, she advised me to do research in folk arts. I promised to do so. Before I returned from Delhi to Madurai Thyagaraja College, I found the local papers had published the photograph of Indira Gandhi talking to me. I continued being the cultural secretary at college. One afternoon, Meera came to see me. His poetry anthology was the prescribed text for M.A. Tamil. Therefore all the students crowded into my room to meet him. I was very proud of that visit.

I invited R.V. Udaiappa, the stage artist, to speak at the college when I was the cultural secretary. He spoke well, and I was appreciated for my choice. When I was in my second year I went away for seventy days to do a diploma in folk theatre from Gandhigram. As a result of which, I could not write the semester exam. It was S.B. Annamalai who sent me for the course, saying, 'Go and learn this art as the ants would collect their food.' That is why, I am today a professor of theatre. I got a first class in M.A. Tamil and secured the first mark at the university level in Saiva Siddhanta. I should thank Meera for this.

When Professor N. Dharmarajan and Meera taught at the Sivaganga Mannar College, they created the Collegiate Teachers Association and fought for the institution to be recognised as a government college. In later days, the association was called MUTA.

7

While I was studying in the Sivaganga Mannar College, I used to be in two minds about going to Elayankudi everytime the college was closed down. At home I cannot expect three meals a day. We had to study with an empty stomach. Even if one was denied regular meals, one still had one's family and friends. One could be in the company of people and places where one had grown up. I would convince myself that nothing was greater than being with these people.

Memories of the race in which I won the champion cup would envelop me as the bus enters Elayankudi, and the high school came into view. I would think about the small groves around the school where Rasula Samudram Wilson and I learnt cinema and devotional songs to the accompaniment of the harmonium. On the left, the DELC Church of Rasula Samudram would be seen, where we used to stage plays during Christmas, and sing songs about the birth of Christ that the priest taught us. The Christian families in turn would give us tea and eats, which we consumed liberally. We would hand over the donations that we collected to the priest.

I remember the time when we used to cycle to the Roman Catholic schools in Puliyadi Thambam, Sarugani, Devakottai, Salaigramam, Sivaganga and other places, singing songs about Jesus set to cinema tunes and distributing economically published booklets of Christmas and New Year songs. There was a Roman Catholic priest in Sivaganga. He lived in the outskirts of the town. If we went to see him during Christmas, he would give us second-hand pants and shirts which were donated by foreigners. The pants and shirts would be altered to fit me, and they made me feel as though I had new clothes for Christmas and New Year.

On the right was the Elayankudi market place. As the bus sped through this area I recalled memories of drinking five paise worth of payasam, eating raw mangoes and picking up tamarind fruits on the way to school. We would hide the tamarind and later sell it at Moolthadian shop. Similarly, we would collect neem seeds and sell them when we had collected enough. I also remembered the treks from Salaiyur hostel to Elayankudi High School. When I recollect all this, I realise that poverty and youth have run like parallel rail tracks in my life.

Books used to be given free of cost to those who studied B.A. Economics in the regional language Tamil. I used to walk from Elayankudi-Salaiyur to Pudhur canal reading a book on the way. Everyday I used to see a girl called Soundram going from Elayankudi to Kannamangalam with the books in her hand and walking at a fast pace. I would console myself that my situation was much better than hers as she had to walk three to four miles everyday to get her education. The Muslim population was large in Elayankudi-Pudhur area. Muslim girls would drop out of school, the moment they attained puberty. It was a big thing for them to even study upto the eighth standard. They did not value education greatly. Even the boys wouldn't show keen interest in attending college after school. Hence, it attracted the attention of many in Salaiyur to find a girl walking such distance to get to school from sixth standard to SSLC. In fact one could tell even the time by observing the girl walking to her school everyday. Upto Pudhur there was a tar road on which buses never plied. From Pudhur to Kannamangalam it was only a mud path.

I had observed the girl for a long time; later I came to know that she was related to me. Whenever Soundram came from Kannamangalam to see my father regarding her studies, she would bring millet, wheat, maize, rice, flour and groundnut. The rice that she brought provided sustenance when there was nothing else at home to eat. Soundram had a soft-spot for me, but I was determined to continue with M.A. ever since my undergraduation at Sivaganga. Though I too was interested in Soundram and was thankful to her for helping us in our poverty ridden days, I stayed away from the temptation to marry her as I had a goal in mind.

I would send a letter to my parents informing them of my trip home from Sivaganga. There were two or three buses going to Elayankudi from Sivaganga everyday. Either father or mother would come to the bus stand to take me home. Mother would ask my father to accompany me if I went out alone at night. If I was late getting home, father and mother would come in search of me. They would be panic-stricken if I was delayed, as they were worried for me. They feared I would be dragged into a fight out of sheer jealousy by people who were not much interested in education.

During the exams, the hostel mess at the Sivaganga College would be closed. My friend Samidoss stayed in the hotel and paid for his food and lodging until the exams got over. His sister's husband had a vegetable shop in Jayamangalam. He would visit Sivaganga without fail to pay mess fees, hostel fees, exam fees, etc. I used to then think that Dalits would do well if they took to business. I was one of those Dalits who completely depended on the scholarship. While doing his M.A. second year, Samidoss got married to his sister's daughter as a mark of gratitude to the family. Now he works for the Electricity Board in Karaikudi.

During the third year final exam, I was not in a position to stay in a hotel to study for the exam. Mother made tamarind rice for me that was supposed to tide me over for four to five days. For two days I consumed it, studied for my exam and wrote my exam too. On the third day the rice got spoilt. Since there was no other go, I threw away the part that had fungus and ate the rest. The last paper was on the fourth day. I started purging and bleeding. I went to the doctor, took medicines and still wrote the morning and afternoon exams in great difficulty. I wore a vetti over my underpants and then wore my trousers on top of it. I wrote the exams even as I was purging. Even now it looks like a miracle that

I wrote my exams in such a state. If I had not written the exam and passed, my life would have taken a different turn.

After the exam got over I came back to Elayankudi. The tamarind rice made by my mother with lot of care had caused amoebeosis, and I was almost on the verge of death. If no one had taken care of me for another day, I would have died. Fortunately for me, Devasigamani Chithappa, who came to visit us saw me in the terrible state and immediately got me admitted at the Rajaji Government Hospital at Madurai.

When I left home for Madurai Hospital, I hugged and kissed my little sisters and wept. People gave me a tearful send off wondering if I would ever get back alive.

The moment I reached the big hospital, Muniyandi Machan took over. He was then a house surgeon there. He reassured me saying, 'Hey, now that you've come to me why do you worry?' In the next few minutes I was given glucose intravenously. Every four hours I had to take a handful of tablets. Next day my father came down to Madurai. After four or five days they took me back to Elayankudi. My sisters, Kalavathi and Malati, and Mother came to the bus stand to take me home. In short, I had touched the edge of death and was back. From that day onwards, I have been scared of eating tamarind rice. For all my troubles, poverty had been the fundamental reason. I had to struggle against poverty to get educated. Even today many young men who come from Dalit families are like me, struggling to escape the clutches of poverty.

When we were residing in a house on Kodikarapattarai Street of Salaiyur, something happened. The house next to mine belonged to Mariyam Biwi Periamma. Next to hers was a house which had a well with a pump set in its backyard. Till 10 o'clock in the night I used to read out form some Islamic text to Mariyam Biwi Periamma, Maimoon Biwi Mami and their friends. Often during the holidays, I used to stay reading on the thinnai outside Mariam Biwi Periamma's house. Soundram used to come to that house sometimes. Whenever she came she would bring something from her house for us. In our place the stove used to be lit only once a day. We used to be very happy when Soundram visited us. Mariyam Biwi Periamma would send rice and vegetables to our house.

Periamma asked my mother one day, 'Bhagyam! Why don't we get Soundram and Gunasekaran married?' Mother told her, 'He should finish his studies, take up a job and help his sisters settle in life. If he gets married and goes away like his brother Karunanidhi, what will I do with these girls?'

Mariyam Biwi Periamma would tease Soundram asking her, 'Do you like Gunasekaran?'

On that particular day I was studying at home. Mother, Mariam Biwi Periamma and Soundram were talking on the thinnai. It was exactly three in the afternoon, and just then it happened.

The people of the street raised an alarm, shouting, 'Ya Allah! Somebody lift him. Get the rope. My god! The child! The child!' Hearing the shouts, I ran out to see what was the trouble. People were running towards Maimoon Mami's house. I too joined them. The women crowded around the well. I made my way through the crowd and peeped into the well. Inside the well was a five-year-old holding the pump set pipe and weeping. Young girls were shaken and cried to Allah for help. Mother and Soundram were speechless. People started saying, 'Get a rope. Get a ladder. Go to the market place and ask the men to come.' The child who had fallen into the well had already drunk lots of water. In a little while it would faint, leave its hold and drown. This thought made me take off my clothes and get into the well in my underpants. I slid down holding the pipe, and the next minute caught hold of the child.

The child had almost fainted. A bucket tied to a rope was sent down. I made the child sit in the bucket. The bucket went up and I kept looking at the child and the bucket. The child was lifted to safety the moment it reached the top.

I found it difficult to come up because the pipe was slippery. Holding on to the pipe and the rope I tried to climb up. I slipped again. However I tried again and managed to climb out of the well. I have never been scared of water. I had the experience of swimming for hours together at the Pavadi pond in my younger days.

Mother took the vetti and helped me get dry. All those gathered around said, 'The child has been taken to the doctor. Take Gunasekaran also to the doctor.' I said no and asked if the child was alright. Mariyam Biwi Periamma caressed me fondly, and said, 'That child survived by Allah's mercy. Not even a single bruise on its body. Had you delayed even a little we would not have had it back alive. Inshaa Allah! Gunasekara, you will be blessed.' She brought out a Singapore balm and applied it on the bruises in my palms and legs.

In the evening many came home from the Jamaat, after finishing their prayers. They said they had come to thank and appreciate Azhagan Teacher's son, Gunasekaran. Father sent them away saying, 'This is something that a human being must do for another. We are not fit to be human beings if we do not do so. You don't have to thank him for it.' But the Jamaat people said, 'Gunasekaran should study in our Dr. Zakir Hussain College. We would give him all the financial help from the Jamaat when he joins PUC.' They helped me as they had promised.

Poverty shadowed our younger days. Father's salary alone was not enough for our school, college expenses and for feeding us. Mother didn't stay at home without doing anything. Father was a teacher. Therefore she tried to earn money keeping in mind the fact that his dignity should not suffer. She would sell firewood to the Muslim households. With the money she earned thus, she would meet the family expenses. Those at home never knew when mother went out and when she came back. I was often her helper in her work. She used to take me along while going to chop firewood. 'Look boy, you come there and study. After I cut the wood and bundle it, you can help me carry it', she would say and take me with her.

With a tin trunk on her head, Mother had in her younger days walked to Elayankudi, and from there to Paramakudi Railway Station to take the train to Ramanathapuram where she stayed in the hostel run by the white people of Schwartz School. She had studied upto eighth standard, which was considered a big qualification in those days. She was offered many government jobs, but we were all very small children and Father did not want my mother to take up a job. Mother who was not used to farm work was now reduced to cutting firewood. If I offered to do her work she would say, 'You go and study. After I make the bundle you can help me lift it to my head.' As she cut the thorn trees she would sing quietly the songs of lamentation rueing her fate. I would pay attention to her songs, but I would never fully understand my mother's soulful keenings. Mother never liked watching movies. Sometimes, after issuing tickets to the women in the cinema tent, Mother might have watched a movie. After she stopped doing this job, Mother never saw movies.

Muslim ladies never wore flowers in their hair. Because of her friendships with them mother too never wore flowers. I have never seen her with flowers or with a bindi on her forehead. Mother never went out to the market or elsewhere without covering her head.

One day Mother took me with her to cut firewood close to the canal at Pudhur. There is a Muslim burial ground close to this place. That place was dense with palmyra trees and thorn bushes.

It was quite hot that day. Mother's hands and legs bled because of the thorns. Just then there came a big cobra. As Mother was chopping a branch from the thorn bush the snake opened its hood, poised to attack her. Mother threw the sickle away, and came running to take me in her arms saying, 'Oh my son'. But even as we looked, the cobra slithered away and disappeared. Mother went back to chopping the wood after drinking a little bit of rice water that she had carried with her in a vessel. After she bundled the firewood, she asked me to lift it up to her head. I too held my breath and tried to lift it up. I was not able to lift it because the bundle was rather big.

We looked around for anyone who might come that way to ask for help. We could not see anyone going either to Pudhur or Elayankudi. Not even a tiny tot was seen along that path that day. Dusk was fast approaching. I said, 'Mother, we will make the bundle into two. You carry one and let me carry the other and let us go home.' Mother caressed me fondly, kissed my cheeks and wept silently as she split the bundle. I lifted the bigger bundle onto her head. Then I placed a cloth on my head and tried to lift up the smaller one. We both started towards the house.

I shoved my books inside my shirt and walked with the bundle on the head. Mother made me go in front and walked behind. We went to the Muslim house to whom mother had already promised the firewood. We put down the bundle there and mother took the money they gave her. I would often think about how we encountered a cobra while collecting firewood. The incident reminds one of the proverb, 'You strive to dig a well but end up letting out a ghost.'

'You must study well, otherwise you will get it with the broom. If the Muslim boys don't study they would set up a shop or go abroad to make a living. If you don't study well, having been born a Paraya you would have to go to somebody else's farm, take care of their cattle, be addressed by them without respect and work like a dog for them. If you study you can live in a dignified manner. So study hard, and whatever you have read, try to think about it with closed eyes. Only then you will remember it when you write your exams.' These are the words that Mother would often say to us to make us come up in life.

The Muslims were very canny businessmen. They would work in some shop even when young. With that experience they would start their own business. Some of the Muslim boys who studied with me have opened their own shops. Some of them went away to Singapore, Malaysia, Saudi Arabia and other countries.

There was a boy called Farook. He was close to me when I was around ten or twelve years old. He was never regular to school. I too lagged behind in studies during that time because of his company.

The Manjaputhur Chettiars and the Aryavysya Chettiars had provision stores in Elayankudi and Salaiyur. Their shops had plenty of gunny bags containing sugar, tamarind and flour. They would give us four annas per bag if we wash and dry them. Farook used to do that and make money that way. With the money thus collected he would go to see M.G.R and Sivaji movies as soon as they were released at Paramakudi or Ramanathapuram. He would take me along at times to see the movies and he seemed to have plenty of money. I would go with him without informing mother. Though I knew I would be beaten up when I went back home, I would be lured by his words and would go away with him. He would tell me stories if I asked him about the money. I still remember the Villupuram story that he told me.

He wanted to travel to Madras from Paramakudi without buying a ticket. He got off at the Villupuram junction and went into the town, wanting to appease his hunger before boarding the train to Madras. Someone had parked his motorbike in Farook's view, taken out a big bag, from which he took a small leather bag and locked it inside the side-box of the bike. After he went away, Farook used a duplicate key to open his side-box and made away with the bag that had more than two thousand rupees. He came back to Elayankudi travelling ticketless.

I went to Ramanathapuram with him to see Sivaji's film *Deiva Magan*. I told Mother all about his theft under the impact of the beatings that I received from her. My thighs, legs, hands, all became red with welts. I let go of his friendship and started concentrating on studies after Mother told me, 'If you are friendly with a rogue, you will also end up in jail.' After a while I came to know that Farook was indeed sent to jail. I sighed with relief and thought that if only mother had not punished me in such a severe manner, I too would have been in jail.

Now and then people on bullock carts would go down our

streets advertising the latest cinema. The songs were broadcast over the mike, and cinema notice would be thrown on the roads. I would pick it up, show it to father at home and would tell him that in such a movie Sivaji had acted out a Shakespearean play or Kovalan Kannagi story or Kattabomman's story, and try to make him understand how cinema had many things related to our studies. Father would then be amenable to giving us money to see the movies.

Father was keen on taking his children to good movies and plays. He would read the *Thirukural* often and explain its meaning at the teachers' forum. He also used to take part in the teachers' movements. Once when the Teachers' Union took a cycle procession from Madurai to Madras he took part in it. Because he brought us up paying attention to arts, literature, politics and education, we too developed an interest in all these things. He encouraged us to take part in all kinds of competitions like poetry reading, singing, acting, public speech and sports activities. Father and mother treasured the prizes that we won. Even when there was nothing for the next meal, Father would be writing petitions on behalf of people who came from nearby villages, or reading, writing or taking notes for his classes without worrying much about food. If he went out, we would wait for him patiently hoping that some way would be found for our food. Father and I used to go in the early hours of Sundays to places in and around Elayankudi like Chitoorani, Kaloorani, and Edayavalasai, etc. Father's students would be in the fields. They would give brinjals, chilies, pumpkins and bottle gourds. During Pongal and Deepavali days we would drain the water in the canals and ponds and collect the fish. Now and then Father would tell us the stories from the Ramayana and Mahabharata. Father was a progressive thinker. Our parents never showed any special interest in God, temples and rituals. We too never came under the influence of faith because of them.

8

I have read that poverty in youth is a very harrowing experience. My early life experiences certainly confirm this belief. My annan and I used to go to Rajamani Akka and Thomas Machan's house in Madurai Pasumalai during our holidays. In Pasumalai, food was served only two times a day – morning and night. There was no food in the afternoon. Akka had two daughters – Jaya and Vasantha, and three boys.

We would reach Pasumalai via Madurai – I have been amazed by the number of cars and buses that raced down that road. I had counted them by hundreds. There were only one or two buses to Elayankudi and we only had the Jaya Vilas bus service. In Pasumalai I would make myself comfortable under a tree and sing through the day. When Thomas Machan had to work on the night shift in the mill, he would take us the next day to angle for fish at the Thiruparankundram lake. We would get lots of fish, and we'd bring them home to make a curry for our dinner. I used to wait outside the mill-gate with the lunch box for him. When the bell goes, Machan would come out and take it from me. One day there was a sudden downpour of rain accompanied by strong winds – the drumstick trees in Akka's and her neighbour's backyard fell down. Vasantha and I bundled the drumsticks and the leaves, went to Pazhanganatham and hawked them in the streets. I used to yearn to go to Pasumalai just to see the buses that speeded towards Madurai.

During April–May holidays, father took us to Erandam Pullikat. When our bus crossed places like Pattukottai, Peraoorani, etc., one would see coconut trees, mango trees and green fields all around. It was in Erandam Pullikat that Muniyandi Machan's brother Malaikannu (alias Madavan) lived. He used to have a brick kiln where he would cut the bricks, bake them and sell them at Mallipattanam and Adhirama Pattanam where Muslims were a majority. My father used to take me there to cut the bricks. Jayaraj (alias) Thyagarajan, Malaikannu Machan's brother, and I, along with another ten or twenty people, would prepare the previous evening, a mixture of silt and river sand mixed with enough water to cut not less than 10000 bricks the next day. The next morning, this mixture would be in the right condition for cutting.

Even now there is a scar in my left hand little finger, where it joins the palm. The scar is the identity mark of the times when I carried the aanja thattu. This instrument is a plate in which the mixture for cutting bricks would be poured upto the capacity of ten spade measure. One load of the aanja thattu would make fifty bricks. A single person can cut upto 1000–2000 bricks in a matter of two or three hours.

Early in the morning, cousin Jayaraj and I would go to the tea shop and drink tea from a vattai. Whoever drank from such cups could easily be identified as Dalits. We could work at the kiln regardless of the hunger pangs till eight or ten having just had tea. Having kanji after this would be divine and the experience would equal nothing else. Later, both of us would go to have toddy. In the afternoon after having a bath and drinking kanji again, we would drift into sound sleep the moment we lay down.

If we planned to watch a movie at Pattukottai or Peraoorani, we would get the brick mixture ready by 4 o'clock that evening. Some days I would go with Malaikannu Machan to the Mallipattinam beach. We would buy big fish and ask Kaliamma Akka to cook it for us. We would have a good meal only at night.

Kaliamma Akka was affectionate towards me and my father. Schools reopen in June. Akka and Machan would send me off with money, rice, new vetti and shirt. The money would be used to meet my sisters' expenses. From Erandam Pullikat to Tanjavur it was just two hours by bus. It was in Tanjavur Reddipalayam that Seenivachgam Anna and Ranjitham Akka resided. Seenivachagam had a good physique. It was my mother who brought him up with care after his own mother passed away. It was she who got his sister in Kaalayaarkoil married too. And so Seenivachagam was very affectionate to mother and me. My relatives would say, that if he took his nayandi nayanam in his hand all those women who danced the karagattam would have a tough time keeping up with him. It is under his leadership that the nayandi melam troupe travelled through Tanjavur. His troupe was highly respected. In those days many from places like north and south Keeranoor, Salaigramam and Ramanathapuram, went north to Tanjavur where they played the nayandi melam and danced karagattam to live in a dignified manner. It was due to Seenivachagam's efforts that the collector allotted a place for the artists to build their houses.

All recall with great pride that it is because of Seenivachagam Annan's efforts that for over three generations people have been able to reside in Mettu Street in Reddipalayam near Tanjavur Medical College. Anna used to get a lot of offers during the season. All the artists playing thavil, pambai, othoodi kuzhal, orumi, thamakku, jalra, nayanam, etc., would be looking upto brother for opportunities. The karagattam dancers would also try to be nice to him. During the season time, he would be playing most nights at Tanjavur, Pattukottai, Pudukottai, Aranthangi, Kumbakonam, Thiruvaroor, Mayiladuthurai and other places. This was the time when the waters of the Cauvery would flow to facilitate the agriculture in Lower and Upper Tanjavur. Seenivachagam toured the area to play nayandi melam for the temple functions, family rituals, marriages and for karagattam artists.

The Parayars who lived in the Mettu Street of Reddipalayam were from Ramanathapuram and Sivaganga regions. Many from these areas had converted to Christianity, and so they had Christian names like Seenivachagam, Arulandu and Devaraj. This is why they built a church in Reddipalayam. They would celebrate Christmas as well as Deepavali. The street was called Mettu Street because the land that was allotted to them by the minister was once part of the upper banks of River Cauvery. They seldom went to the Medical College side. If they walk along the river for two kilometres, they would reach Tanjavur town. Even then they would rent out rooms near the Tanjavur bus stand and stay there. They would do so in order to get hold of clients who came in search of artists, thereby eshewing the interference of the agents. One can see the artists in and around the Tanjavur bus stand itself anytime of the day.

If Tanjavur is still famous for karagattam it is because of the Parayars, who have settled down in Mettu Street from Sivaganga and Ramanathapuram areas. Seenivachagam Annan's pipes were embellished with gold lockets. Impressed by the golden trinkets, many would immediately give an advance for his performance considering him a famous artist. His remuneration would thus go up. The artists who performed the nayandi melam were all from Mettu Street. They would wash their shirts and vettis in the river and dress up smart. One has to make a special mention of their expertise at laundering their clothes. Seenivachagam Annan had rented out the front room of a house next to Muniyandi Hotel, behind the bus stand.

Once I came all alone, from Erandam Pullikat to Tanjavur by bus. People in the bus stand took me to Annan's quarters when I enquired about him. It was season time for him. He took me to the big temple and showed me around. He introduced me to the fellow artists saying, 'This is my younger brother, doing B.A. in college. No one can equal him in singing.' After getting back to his lodgings he asked the people around to look after me as he had to go away on one of his performance tours. He gave me twenty rupees and introduced me to the owner of Muniyandi Hotel, asking him to provide for my meals. He left asking me to stay in his room.

One day the Mettu Street artists asked me to sing. They

appreciated me after listening to my song. They told me, 'There is one karagattam dancer here. She is a good singer. She charges an amount for her dance. But she would also impress people with her song and earn an equal amount by way of presents that people give her. You should sing in her presence tomorrow and bring her down a peg or two. We will go and tell her now itself that you will come tomorrow.'

Next day, they took me to the karagattam dancer Mallika's house near the northern gate. She was expecting me and she welcomed me saying, 'Anna come, Mama come, Sir do come in'. She took us inside her house and gave us tea.

It looked like she had just then spat out the betel leaves that she had munched on. She was decked with gold on her ears and nose. Dark complexioned, she was of good height too. On the walls were her photographs and the prizes she had won. Here and there one could see the karagattam costumes, karagattam pot, wig, etc., revealing that it was the house of a good artist. Mallika kept saying to a girl standing next to her – another karagattam dancer, 'Go and buy betel leaves... Spread the mat there... Why are you standing? Go and sit somewhere there...' etc. The girl did whatever she told her to do.

Those who came with me whispered in my ears that she was Mallika's lover. I grew faint on hearing this. I just could not believe that a woman could marry another woman.

The Tamizh Sangam had invited me to U.S.A to felicitate Sivaji Ganesan when he had received the Chevaliar Award. I went to Canada also. Over there I saw around 40000 people taking part in a procession demanding the legislation of same sex marriages. I was reminded of Mallika in Tanjavur.

'You are Seenivachagam Mama's thambi, is it? I am proud of having an educated boy like you coming to my house. All these people told me that you sing very well. Please sing a song for me, I am eager to listen,' said Mallika.

'I heard that you sing very well. In fact, I came to hear your voice. I have come in search of you and therefore you should sing first. I will sing after you', I replied.

Mallika smiled and kept looking at the ceiling thoughtfully for a little while. She chose to sing the song, 'Within the seven swaras, how many ragas …' This was from a recently released movie and was a difficult song with a variety of beat and humming sequences. Mallika sang the song and I applauded her performance with all the others. Her choice of song showed that she invited me to a challenge.

'Sir! I sang because you asked me to. It's your turn now,' Mallika said. I sang a verse from *Abhirami Andadhi*, that Muniyandi Machan had taught me. It began with the lines:

> Unshaken knowledge,
> Undiminishing riches…

The song had a scope for raga and pitch variations. I finished singing. The drum players and the dancers residing in the street crowded in front of Mallika's house on listening to my song. They appreciated my song and enquired about my background. They got me tea. One person in fact slipped a ten rupee note into my shirt pocket and slapped me on my shoulder. Mallika fell at my feet, 'I have not heard such a voice in my life. When this Mama and Annan told me about you, I never expected you to have such expertise. You must come to watch my dance at the big temple tomorrow.' I was secretly thrilled to go to the big temple once again. The very look of the temple used to scare me. Every time I went into the temples which had a gopuram, my heart would race with fear as I wondered whether they would allow a low-caste into the temple. The panic would grip me until I leave the temple – I feared I would be beaten up for entering the temple. I would remember with unease the two times that I had gone to the Kaalaiyaar Temple.

The next evening, I went to the big temple at Tanjavur. I looked at the gopuram from a distance. It had a figure wearing the sacred thread stamping another figure under its feet. The dark figure which had its tongue out resembled me. Each sculpture on the gopuram had a story behind it. Seeing such terrible stories depicted on it, I was scared of entering it all by myself. Many went to see the temple and many came out too. I took courage and went in. However I waited for a long time outside the entrance of the gopuram fearing that from my face itself I would be identified as a Paraya. Just then Arulandu Annan came by. 'What's up thambi? Come let us go in,' he said. 'Will they allow us in?' I asked. For which he replied, 'Unless our people play the drums first, the drum inside the temple will not be played. It is our people who will lead the procession of the deity by playing the parai. Without us the deity will not go on a procession.' So saying he took me inside the temple.

We went inside and slept on the soft grass. By about 8 o'clock in the night Seenivachagam Annan came in with his nayanam. Along with him came the nayandi melam troupe. He enquired, 'Thambi did you eat? Dei, go and get parota and mutton for brother.' Anna sent a drummer with money to get me some food. I asked, 'Where are the dancers? Will Mallika dance today?' I was told that she would arrive shortly in an auto after her make-up.

'Will our people be allowed inside the temple?' I asked.

Anna said, 'We are allowed up till here. We cannot go inside the sanctum sanctorum where the deity resides.'

Not bad, I thought. They have allowed us to enter at least till here even after knowing who we are. The tinkling bells of the dancer's anklets were heard. Mallika came with four or five other karagattam dancers. My parota and mutton parcel came. I wanted to know if we were allowed to eat inside the temple. 'You just eat. Who is going to ask you? Eat', said one of them, and I ate. Mallika paid her respects by touching the feet of Seenivachagam Annan and others with him. The other dancers also followed suit. They also paid their respect to the various instruments like thaval, nayanam, pambai, urumi, thamuku, othoodi kuzhal, etc. Finally they paid obeisance to the earth and the presiding deity of the temple.

Mallika greeted me as I was eating. She spoke to Seenivachagam

Annan, praising me sky-high. It was then 10 o'clock in the night. The deity came out for a procession. The nayandi melam and karagattam was performed in front of the temple. There was an elderly gentleman who was assisting Mallika. As she danced, he poured out something for her every now and then from a vessel in his hand. The deity started its procession around the city. The nayandi melam troupe and the karagattam dancers performed in front of the procession. At every street corner the dancers would increase their tempo. I kept wondering about what was being offered to Mallika after every dance or a song. I asked the old man who accompanied her about this. He laughed and enquired if I was Seenivachagam's brother. I nodded my head in assent.

'It's country liquor', he said and put it under my nose. I could smell the strong odour of the liquor. Arulandu and I left thinking that we had seen enough of the dance.

'If you play pambai or thamuku you will get not less than 150 rupees per day. Will you come tomorrow? We will join some troupe and start playing', said Arulandu Annan. I said yes and also added that I didn't know much about playing these instruments. 'If you pose for two days as though you are playing, on the third day you will learn', he said. I tried playing the thamuku in Annan's place. One of my machans there taught me how to hold it in my hand and play fast. I also wanted to try my hand on playing the pambai. Immanuel Annan told me that it was enough to strum it with the two sticks in the right hand held between the thumb and the index finger. I tried playing it for two days whenever I had time. The third day, I went with Arulandu to play the jalra with the group of drummers – that's when the problem came up.

'Why didn't the person we had booked come? How can we accept someone who has been sent by Mallika when she has taken the advance for the performance?'

The problem was becoming too much to handle and it looked

as though the programme would not take place. The elder of the group, who took the advance, was helpless. Arulandu and I looked at each other wanting to put an end to the problem and go ahead with the programme. He had studied upto SSLC and was expecting orders for a police job. The girls who had come to dance karagattam were bewildered. It was sad to see the artists in such a condition. Two big men of the village said, 'All of you get into the car. There won't be any dance today. Unless you bring the person to whom we gave the advance, there won't be any programme.'

I took the two aside and spoke to them. They then said, 'Ok! Let them dance. Why should we prevent those who have come for dancing? Ok! Let them play the drums and begin the programme.' The drummers and the dancers were surprised. They appreciated my intervention saying, 'Seenivachagam's thambi has convinced them and has got us this assignment. He has studied in a college, that is why he has spoken in the right way and solved the problem'.

The elderly gentlemen, who had taken the advance, held my hand and thanked me. Arulandu Annan asked me what I had said to make them change their minds. Two of the drummers joined us and also wanted to know what I had told them. I told the artists, 'Alright! Go and eat. Girls you should start doing your make-up.' I called the girl who had come in the place of Mallika, and told her, 'Look here, I have said much about you. We must get a good name and it all depends upon your performance. All of us should be at our best today.' Everyone went away to eat.

Arulandu, who is now a sub-inspector, asked me again, 'Thambi Gunasekara! How did you solve the problem?' I told him I assured them saying, 'Ayya! The girl for whom you gave the advance should not come to your village. You will be polluted. Mallika is menstruating. Even if she comes to dance she won't be able to dance upto your expectation. Please watch the dance of the girl who has come in her place. Pay us afterwards if you are satisfied with the performance. Those who have come to dance in your village today have danced in Delhi and in the cinema. You will want the same girl to dance in your temple festival next year also. You will listen to excellent reproductions of folk songs and cinema songs.' I told Arulandu Anna that I had mixed a little untruth to my reasoning and that is how the problem got solved. I was a little worried. I sat next to the dancer and told her how and where she should sing folk songs and cinema songs and when she should sing with me.

That day the nayandi melam started in an upbeat mood. The moment the karagam was put down, I took the mike and sang a folk song:

> In the open pond of Vellalars,
> In the cucumber garden,
> You said I touched you,
> And went to a distance –
> I said I am your own sweet heart –
> You stood mesmerised

I received not only claps but also gifts from the people around when I finished singing.

I played thamuku and pambai. Then the dancer girl and I sang songs challenging each other. Then we had a Kuratti dance, buffoon strip, etc., and the people sat up till early in the morning enjoying our show. When we finished the programme successfully, they said, 'We want the same troupe next year also.' The village heads wished us success and gave us a little more money than what we had asked for and sent us away with great respect. That Mallika had gone to some other village to dance for a better payment was known to me only the next day.

It was the end of the summer holidays. I had collected enough money for the college fees, hostel fees, etc. I came back to Elayankudi. The one month I spent in the company of folk artists was an important experience in my life.

Irudayaraj and Subburaj worked for the Sivaganga Telephones. Subburaj used to play the base guitar and Irudayaraj the main guitar. They had a group of artists who sang light music and cine music. I joined as a singer in their troupe and practised in the evening. Gangabalan Annan sang in Chandrababu's voice. I took practice for T.M.S and Seerkazhi Govindarajan's voices. I went to sing in many places like Devakottai, Karaikudi, Sivakasi, Madurai and Sivaganga. I used to get anywhere between fifty to two hundred and fifty rupees. I used to get invitations on and off to sing in the Madurai Modern Orchestra. They would send a car to take me to places like Madurai, Chozhavandan and Thirumangalam, and I would come back with garlands and money. I have helped my friends with the money thus earned while in college. Temple festivals would coincide with the the final exams in the month of March and April. I had to refuse some offers as I had to study for my exam. I had sung with the then famous Malaysian singers Chandra and Indra. I received the acclamation of the audience by singing old cinema songs like – *Mullai Mallar Mele* and the latest songs like *Paruthi Edukayila Enna Palla Nalla Patha Machan*.... Once on a stage in Chozhavandan, I sang a folk song:

> Oh my lady! The light of the moon and sun,
> Would start from the sandal hill,
> In the dead of night – I want to,
> Make you mine,
> O my picture-perfect darkling!
> You saree clad lady,
> I have no sleep – verily,
> I lack sleep – thoughts of the bindi on your forehead,
> And your bosom gladdens my heart,
> Oh! It gladdens my heart.

The song was received well and I got a lot of gifts. From then onwards I sang folk songs in between movie songs on the stage. I received good response and appreciation whenever I did that. That made me toy with the idea of starting a troupe which sang only folk songs. During my final-year B.A. vacation, before joining M.A., my pre-university teacher, Shajahan Kani, introduced me to Gandarvan, Parambai Selvan and M. Jameson of Paramakudi. We put up plays written by Parambai Selvan and directed by

Shajahan Gani. Gandarvan and Comrade S.A.P helped us stage plays at the women's conferences, writer's conferences and trade-wing associations. I had previous experience of having scored music for Karunanidhi Annan and Muniyandi Machan's production *Erukuttam Parkiren.*

Comrade Jameson arranged for my performance at the Tamil Nadu progressive writer's forum at Singanampuri in Sivaganga. Gandhi Annavi played the nadaswaram and Duraisingam, with a missing finger, played the thavil. Azhgarswami Teacher and Gangaibalan helped by playing the Pambai and Urumi, and writing the lyrics and setting it to music. It is with the help of all these people that I staged the first folk music show. In that performance I sang:

> What is this, O deity Jakamma? The world,
> Is hanging upside down – is it right?

I also sang the song written by T.V. Pachaiappan about the cotton mill workers which goes –

> Having come to work for the cotton mill,
> We are being blown like cotton itself – Oh Sir,
> Having worked tirelessly,
> We are a scrap of what we were.

We also sang poet Inquilab's song:

> Human Beings! We are human beings,
> Like you, like him.
> We too are human beings,
> Our bones and flesh bake in the fire lit by you,
> Your government and court,
> Pouring oil on it.
> You keep declaring this and that as allowance –
> When we were all burning down,
> whose hair,
> did you go to pluck?

This song of Inquilab's is apt even today. And there is still a need for the performances of my Thanane troupe.

Select Glossary

Ammayi	Maternal grandmother
Annan	Elder brother
Appam	Rice preparation, similar to Dosai, but thicker in the centre
Athai	Father's sister
Ayya	Sir
Chachi	Aunt (term generally used by Muslims influenced by Urdu)
Chakiliyar	An aboriginal agricultural community. Chakiliyar's work with leather, and are considered untouchables. They are also know by the term Arundathiyar.
Cheri	A settlement outside the village where the Schedule castes live, something like a ghetto
Chettiars	A caste Hindu community, usually involved in trading
Chithappa	Father's younger brother
Cinamma	Mother's sister or father's second wife
Dosai	A kind of pancake made with fermented rice flour batter.
Gopuram	Temple tower
Idli	Steamed food made with rice flour
Jalra	Cymbals, used to keep time to music
Kabadi	A kind of team-game.
Kaili	A garment for men made with a piece of cloth sewn together in the ends. Usually made with bright-coloured cloth with a floral or checkered pattern.
Kanji	Gruel
Karagattam	An acrobatic folk dance in which the dancer bears a flower-decked, water-filled pot on her head.
Karnam	A village officer who maintains the record of land revenue.

Kavadi	A folk dance form performed with a wooden semi-circular structure that is usually decorated with peacock feathers.
Kitti	The game of tip-cat
Koothu	Folk theatre
Konar	An agricultural caste Hindu community. Konars generally tend to goats and cows.
Kottumelam	A common name for percussion instruments.
Kudukudupaikaran	A soothsayer, who usually announces his presence and punctuates his predictions by playing a drum-like rattle.
Machan	Son of one's maternal uncle or paternal aunt; also, refers to wife's brother or sister's husband.
Machi	A relationship term
Mama	Mother's brother
Mami	Aunt (maternal uncle's wife)
Masi	Eleventh month of the Tamil calendar, mid-February to mid-March
Namaz	Prayer
Nayanam	A long wind instrument
Nayandi melam	An ensemble of musical instruments accompanying folk dances like karagattam and kavadi.
Othoodi kuzhal	A long wind instrument used as an accompaniment.
Pambaram	Top
Panangkizhangu	A kind of root vegetable
Panniyaram	A snack made of rice flour and jaggery.
Parayar	An aboriginal agricultural community. Parayars were forced to do menial jobs like burning the dead, and are considered untouchables.
Pathaneer	Palmyra sap collected in a pot lined with lime to prevent fermentation.
Periamma	Mother's elder sister
Periappa	Mother's elder sister's husband or father's elder brother
Poori masal	Food item made by frying wheat dough in oil, and served with a potato curry.
Sambar	A kind of gravy prepared by adding condiments, vegetables and tamarind paste to cooked lentils.
Sami	Expression of respect

Sundal	Boiled and spiced pulses, served as snacks.
Sunnath	Circumcision ceremony
Thali	The sacred thread tied around the neck of the bride during a marriage ceremony.
Thamaku	A kind of small drum used as a tom-tom
Thambi	Younger brother
Thapattai	A small drum, hung around the shoulders and played with a pair of small sticks.
Tharai	Long, brass trumpet-like instrument.
Thasildar	Revenue officer in charge of a small division
Thatha	Grandfather
Thavil	A drum played with the hand on one side, and a stick on the other.
Thevar	A martial caste Hindu community.
Thinnai	A small raised platform in the verandah of the house
Uthappam	A thicker variety of dosai to which vegetables are sometimes added.
Uppuma	A common South Indian dish made of semolina
Vattai	a saucer-like vessel
Vetti	White cloth used as a lower garment by men
Vellai	White